DECIMATE

kristin harte

DECIMATE

kristin harte

Chapter One

DEACON

The older I got, the more I realized how much getting older sucked.

Doing my best to stretch out the soreness that came from years of abusing my body, I reached for a phone that I no longer kept on the nightstand. *Fuck.* Nighttime Deacon knew morning Deacon would wake up, stretch, and scroll, looking for messages he shouldn't want. Being disappointed when he didn't receive them in the first place. Nighttime Deacon left the phone across the room, so morning Deacon was forced to crawl out of bed to retrieve the infernal device.

Nighttime Deacon was a bastard, and morning Deacon hated him.

But morning Deacon had a full day of avoiding people, avoiding that same phone, and trying to pretend his life was anything other than the shitshow it had become. Morning Deacon was me, which meant I needed to haul my ass out of my bed and get to it.

"Rise and shine, motherfuckers." I repeated the words I'd heard throughout most of my Army days, the ones that had a surefire way of waking me up and getting my ass in gear. They did what they always had—seven syllables of motivation had me up and running for the shower.

Fine, not running. Sort of...hobbling. But I was getting older by the day, and my old bones were making sure I knew it. Hence the morning shower even after I'd taken one the night before. Had to warm up the muscles.

The hot water definitely woke up my body, but it also woke up my mind. Reminding me of all the ways I had fucked up recently. Not necessarily throughout my life—though there were many moments I could have ruminated on—but just in the last month or so. Say, from Alder's wedding on. More precisely, from two nights before Alder's wedding on. That sinking feeling I kept trying to chase away with avoidance and rye whiskey returned to my gut as it did every morning, that sense of impending doom settling over me. I pictured a smug-as-fuck cloud smirking right there on my shoulders, looking irritatingly happy and almost satisfied. He was just waiting for me to mess up and admit what I'd done, to destroy my life in Justice because of one bad decision. He was waiting for me to tell Alder about that night...

Not that I ever would.

I dried off and headed into my bedroom to toss on faded jeans and a tee, still trying to shake the sick feeling that would never go away. I couldn't tell anyone what I'd done, couldn't relieve myself of the burden of my bad decisions. If I did, I could lose everything. My friends, the people I saw as family, my livelihood, my life.

"They won't actually kill you."

But even saying the words out loud didn't help me believe them. Not a bit.

Fuck me, I needed to get some food and stop being so melodramatic.

I grabbed my phone, still ignoring the damn thing and not obsessively pressing the home button to see if I had any messages I shouldn't want, and headed into my living room. The one that sat in the house I owned and lived alone in. Funny thing, though—I wasn't alone.

"Did you break in to my house to eat my snacks?"

Alder Kennard—best friend, practically my brother, and royal pain in my ass—sat in my favorite recliner with his feet up and a bag of salt and vinegar potato chips by his hip. He kept his eyes on mine as he reached into that bag, grabbed a handful of *my* chips, and shoved them into his mouth. The crunching was like some sort of added bonus, exasperatingly loud and slow to grate just the right way on my nerves.

The trouble with being best friends with someone for most of your adult life was that the man knew exactly how to push your buttons. In true Kennard style, Alder was stomping on mine.

"If you drop one fucking crumb, you're vacuuming." I continued into the kitchen. My coffee sat in the pot untouched, the timer having gone off and the nectar I needed to function having brewed exactly as nighttime Deacon had planned. I guess he wasn't a complete bastard...just enough of one to irritate the fuck out of morning me.

I poured my cup, trying hard not to think about what I shouldn't be thinking about. Fighting the nerves and the unease that Alder now made me feel whenever I saw him. Wishing his wife Shye were with him so I could use her as a distraction. I did so love flirting with the little woman—it annoyed Alder to no end. As if he had anything to worry about there—Shye loved him to the moon and back. And I...well, nighttime Deacon was a bastard, but not a big enough one to mess with his best friend's wife.

Just enough to mess with...others.

Coffee in hand, mind focused on not talking about the things I couldn't stop thinking about, I returned to my living room. Alder had his feet back on the floor, looking serious as usual. The guy was a newlywed, having finally captured the attention of the woman he'd been pining over for years. Why he looked so damn worried was beyond me.

"Shye kick you out already?"

Alder grunted what would likely have been a laugh. "You wish."

I didn't, but keeping Alder Kennard's head size in scale to his body was practically a full-time job—and one that had fallen into my lap when I'd followed him home after we had both retired from the Army Special Forces. His relationship was an easy target.

"You'd better be treating that woman right. Don't think I won't swoop in and replace you if you fuck it up."

"It's not a pageant, Deac. You're not runner-up."

"Says you." I took a sip of my coffee, looking him over. "Why aren't you working today?"

It was Friday, and Alder always worked at his mill on Fridays. No three-day weekends or casual Fridays for that man. Not that I blamed him. The Kennard mill supported most of the families who lived in this little pissant town, which meant Alder had a lot of responsibility on his shoulders. I didn't envy him that.

"I gave the entire mill the week off because of the holiday and started it early—figured I might as well take the time off, too."

The holiday. Right. Thanksgiving was less than a week away.

Which meant people might be coming home to enjoy time with family. Which meant—

I really had to figure out how to stop thinking of her. "You give them all this time off with full pay?"

Those bright-blue eyes—the sharpest ones I'd ever seen outside of the animal world—stabbed through me, his look enough to turn lesser men into panicked sacks of flesh. An eagle on the hunt, a predator locking in on its prey.

"Of course I did. I'm not an asshole."

"The jury is still out on that one."

He sighed and shook his head, chuckling softly. "I have no idea why I put up with you."

I pointed at the abandoned bag of potato chips. "For my snacks, of course. Pass me that bag, boss."

He did as I asked, tossing me the bag of salty, bite-you-back deliciousness. Totally didn't go with the coffee I was still drinking, but I didn't care. If I saw chips, I was eating chips. Period.

"So," I finally said, tired of waiting him out. "Why are you here if not for these chips?"

Alder sighed, shaking his head. "It's been quiet."

I didn't need him to elaborate—I understood exactly where his mind had gone. It'd been quiet since we'd run the Black Angels motorcycle club out of town. We'd been under attack from the Soul Suckers club for months, and they'd sent in their buddies to wear us down even further. That hadn't worked, of course. Two of Alder's brothers and I had made sure of that. Sure, the Soul Suckers had tried again not too long after that, had infiltrated their way into our community and upset the balance, but we'd taken care of that threat, too.

We'd seen nothing of that crew since, which obviously didn't sit well with the big man.

It didn't sit well with me either.

"You think they're going to come back for another go at us." Not a question. Alder and I had been working together on missions for decades—I knew his mind better than he did.

"I do. I think they'll wait for us to be distracted with the holidays and then storm in."

I nodded my agreement. "It's something I'd do. We need to be ready to stop them before they claim a single inch of Justice."

Alder nodded, his face screwing up. "We're going to need to set up more watches, widen our net, and make sure everyone is prepared."

By prepared, he meant armed. Which meant we needed supplies. That was my job.

"I'll take care of that last part."

"Good." He stood up, stretching. Thankfully not touching my ceiling with his greasy hands. "Get yourself set, man. We need to head into town."

"For what?"

"I want to eat, see my woman, and track down Chase. All of which require us to be on Main Street."

I shrugged, moseying my way to the kitchen to pour my coffee into a travel mug. I sealed the potato chip bag and placed it back in the cupboard before washing the grease from my hands. Towel hung up, mug set in the dishwasher to be washed later, and everything exactly where it needed to be, I headed back to the living room. My coat hung on a hook by the back door, my flip-flops and boots underneath it. The juxtaposition of the shoes was a really good metaphor for my life. One all business—if you considered kicking ass and killing people business—the other all relaxation. My *don't fuck with me* and my *no worries* footwear, living in harmony.

Today was a day with worry, though.

Socks on, boots on, jacket on, travel mug in hand, I opened the door and looked back at Alder, who stood in the middle of my living room, watching me.

"Let's go."

Alder nodded. "You're a lot like Finn, you know."

Finn. His younger brother. The one who worked for me. The one who was a recovering addict and had a lot of OCD tendencies he relied on to find peace in a chaotic world. One of the strongest fuckers I'd ever met.

"Thanks. That's the nicest thing you've ever said to me."

Alder drove downtown, not being an asshole for most of the way. Most, not all.

"Don't spill that coffee."

I raised the mug to my lips and took an exaggerated sip, slurping really loud just for him before smacking my lips together. "Not a drop."

His jaw ticked, and I grinned. The morning had truly turned around for me. There was nothing better than hot coffee and getting under Alder's skin. Both at once? A total gift from the universe. One I planned to take full advantage of.

Alder drove like an old man on a Sunday afternoon for some reason, but we eventually made it into town and to the restaurant—The Baker's Cottage. Cute little thing named Katie owned it, and that girl made the best darn soup I'd ever had. There wasn't much that could beat out lunch at the Cottage, except maybe breakfast there. Thankfully, we were right at that time between the two meals, so I could get a cup of soup along with some ham steaks and biscuits.

And coffee—Katie and Shye brewed amazing coffee. Yeah, that whole meal sounded good. Just what a man needed to get his day started right.

But as we walked through the door of the restaurant—bell ringing overhead and everything—the idea of a day started right flew straight out the window. Standing at the counter was a blond woman. Tall, curvy, what kids had started calling thick, with hair that I'd had wrapped around my hand once. With an ass that I'd spanked and grabbed and bit. With legs that I'd been blessed to spend an evening between.

My world skidded sideways as I soaked in the view of parts and pieces of a woman I had no business lusting after. No business whatsoever. Falling for her could destroy my life in an instant, as could the knowledge of the one-night stand we'd had before I'd known who she was becoming public. That woman was hell in heels on a good day.

Today would not be a good day.

"Lainie?" Alder stuttered to a stop, looking almost as surprised as I felt. Especially when the blonde turned and with a smile that slipped the second she spotted me at Alder's side. "Well, what do you know. My baby sister's back in town."

I was so fucked.

Chapter Two

LAINIE

Growing up the youngest—and only—sister in a family already populated with four boys had taught me a lot of things. Kindness, sharing, empathy, the disgusting smell of a teenage boy's room, how much food men could put away, and how to make sure my voice was heard over multiple fights and arguments going on at once. What that experience hadn't taught me was patience.

"Why is this drive taking so long?"

Elijah—brother number four, one of a set of twins, and only one of two I spoke to on a regular basis—huffed and shot me a *will you please stop asking me that question* look.

"It's not taking any longer than usual, Lainie. Sit back, read a book—"

"No."

"Take a nap, then."

"Not tired."

He growled in that adorable way he had a tendency to when I was really bothering him. Living with him for the past few years had taught me a lot, like that his fuse was getting a little too short when he made that sound. Time for a distraction.

"So," I said, dragging out the vowel and turning slightly in my seat so I could see his profile. "You went on a date the other night."

"No."

"No, you didn't go on a date?"

"No, I will not be talking to you about this."

Which meant he'd been on a date. The man was so secretive.

"I tell you about my dates."

He shot me a mean sort of smirk. "What dates? You've been holed up at home studying for months. I swear, you're just pissy at the world because you haven't gotten laid in forever."

I bit the inside of my lip, holding in all the ways he was wrong. I *had* gotten laid and somewhat recently. Just a few weeks prior, while home in Justice, of all places. I'd flirted with, picked up, and taken home the biggest, most amazing and attentive partner I'd ever had. I'd had a one-night stand that had ruined me for all other men.

A one-night stand that could have been more had the guy not been who he was.

Fine, I *was* pissy because I couldn't get laid.

"Thanksgiving is going to suck."

Elijah cocked his head, keeping his eyes on the road. "Why do you say that?"

"One, Alder and Bishop will be there being their usual overbearing selves. Two, I barely know Anabeth and don't really know Shye at all, yet you boys are going to leave me with the womenfolk because god forbid I be allowed to hang with the men."

"You've known Anabeth since we were kids—"

"No, you and Finn knew her. I didn't get to hang with you three."

"Fine, but she's not a stranger, and you know it. Shye, on the other hand, is. But she's really nice—quiet and calm. I like her a lot."

Yeah, so did I, to be honest. Didn't change the fact that I simply didn't *know* her.

But Elijah wasn't done. "I know it's been a year of a lot of changes—"

"You mean half a year. Not even. Everything started going nuts over the summer."

"Fine. Half a year. A handful of months that have brought a lot of changes." He finally looked away from the road, giving me a hard stare that could have frozen me in my tracks. No wonder other lawyers called him the Eagle. "Things were always going to change. Our brothers have grown up. It's about time you did as well."

I had nothing to say back to that because I didn't want to fight with Elijah. He and Finn were the only two I had left. True, Alder was ten years older than me and Bishop just over eight, so Elijah and Finn were much closer to my age. That didn't excuse the years of no contact by the older ones, though. The always treating me like some tagalong in their male-dominated fantasies of how life should be. That didn't make it okay to completely dismiss me.

I'd grow up and stop acting like a brat around them the second they all accepted that I wasn't a little girl anymore.

I kept my mouth shut for the rest of the drive, letting Elijah relax and doing my best not to grow more anxious and irritated as we climbed into the Rocky Mountain Front. Eventually, trees gave way to a town—small but clean, cute but mostly empty. Justice. The place where I'd been born, where I'd grown up, and where three-fifths of my family still lived. It was only Elijah and me who had escaped to the city.

"Main Street looks good," Elijah said, throwing the car into park once he swung into a spot. "I always expect the empty storefronts to look dirty, but they never do. Alder does a good job keeping this place from falling into disrepair."

I didn't vocalize my answer because I didn't feel like heaping praise on to Alder right then. Elijah wasn't wrong, though. Main Street *was* mostly empty, and without a strong hand guiding the town to keep up repairs, the place could have looked more like the rest of the small towns in the area—scary, poor, and half dead. Instead, Justice's Main Street looked as if it had a fresh coat of paint on it, and even the empty stores had functioning lights and clean windows. He took care of our home just fine.

I wouldn't be patting him on the back anytime soon, though.

"I want to stop into Katie's place for lunch. Grab some soup and see what she's been up to." I slipped out of the car and headed for the trunk, knowing Elijah would want to see the apartment where we were staying first.

"Finn's waiting for us at the hardware store," Elijah said, his eyes locked on his phone. "We can drop off our stuff then head over."

The man was nothing if not predictable.

We made our way to the alley entrance of the hardware store, both of us grinning the second we saw Finn.

"At what point do you two start looking more identical?" I hollered, nodding when his own smile spread across his handsome face. "You've bulked up a little—looks good."

Finn hurried to me and wrapped me in a warm hug that was like being snuggled into an electric blanket. The man had always been warm, and I missed his furnace hugs a lot.

"What's up, princess?" He gave me a kiss to the top of my head before turning to Elijah—his twin and best friend. "It's good to see you again so soon."

"How are you doing, Finn?" Elijah hugged his brother, both of them giving each other those manly backslaps that always looked as if they hurt a little.

"Things are good here. Quiet." Finn led the way to the door that would take us to the living area of the hardware store. "Mercy and Beckett are out right now, but she left me the keys for the second unit."

We followed him up the back stairs to the small hallway that had only two doors—one for each apartment over the store. The Bell family had owned the building and run the hardware store for decades, and Mercy had lived over it since she'd come home to help the family business stay afloat. Elijah and I would be staying in the empty unit, seeing as how Justice had no hotels or home rentals. Well, there was the cheap motel attached to the bar on the edge of town, but we wouldn't be looking at that as an option.

"This one's mine," Elijah said as soon as he walked into the apartment, heading right for the bedroom at the back of the place. "You take the front room."

"What if I wanted the back room?"

"You snooze, you lose. I called dibs first."

"He did," Finn said, nodding with a look of utter seriousness on his face. "He called dibs."

Those two would never—and I mean *never*—grow up.

"Fine. But don't go unpacking and setting up your hair station in the bathroom. I need sustenance if you want me to stay my normal, sparkling self."

Finn raised an eyebrow, catching Elijah's eye. "She get hangry?"

"Not yet, but it's coming." Elijah pushed my bag into my room and grabbed my hand, dragging me along after him. "Let's make sure we keep the hungry beast at bay."

The three of us clomped downstairs and around the front of the building, my brothers laughing and joking like always. I soaked it in —the banter, the loudness, the feeling of being home. I didn't waste a single second of feeling like family again. I missed home, missed Justice and the people I grew up with. But Justice would never give me the opportunities a city like Denver did. I'd left to go to college, and I had no plans to return now that I was done. But short visits like this—yeah, those had been missed.

Elijah opened the door for us when we reached The Baker's Cottage—the restaurant owned and run by my best friend from high school. Katie Baker and I had always gotten along really well, and I was looking forward to snagging her for a girls' night out or something. That thought had me running through the other ladies I knew in town. Maybe we could convince Mercy Bell to go along with us. I'd have invited Anabeth, but she was pregnant and being a homebody. I didn't know much about Alder's wife, Shye, but I had a feeling he wouldn't be too fond of me taking her out drinking without him to helicopter around us. Finn had a girl as well—Jinx. She seemed nice and normal. Bet she'd be a fun one to hang with, though Finn's addiction issues made me second-guess that.

Talk about a lot of life changes in a short time for my family. Three out of five...basically locked down and hitched. There was a *baby* on the way. A new Kennard would be joining the ranks. All of which had happened over the summer and into the fall. Meanwhile, I was still in Denver with Elijah, neither of us really even dating much.

I was going to need to mull that over later. And plan that girls' night.

"Lainie!" Katie raced through the door to the kitchen, grinning and looking the exact same as she had in high school. "I'm so glad you're home. I've missed you."

She gave me a big hug, giggling when she pulled away. "There's so much to talk about—you had better set up a night out with just us girls, Miss Planner. I need it."

The woman knew me well. "Absolutely. We'll plot some sort of world domination night at the bar. It'll be just what the doctor ordered."

"I knew I could count on you." She looked over my shoulder as the entrance bell rang, giving me a sorry sort of frown. "I need to get back in the kitchen. Shye will take care of you, okay? Whatever you want—it's on me."

"We're not eating your food without paying," Elijah said, giving her that smooth smile that tended to make women go cross-eyed. "I'm pretty sure Gage would not think highly of us if we took advantage of you like that."

Katie giggled again. "He's so overprotective. You guys enjoy your lunch—we'll deal with the tab when the time comes."

And with that, she spun and hurried off into the kitchen, slipping under the arm of the big, burly man who tended to always be with my brother Bishop. Gage—Katie's boyfriend and Bishop's partner in crime. No doubt, he'd be letting my brother know we were home and in town within a few minutes. There was no escaping the watchful eyes in Justice.

The three of us took over a table in the far corner, me facing the door, while Elijah and Finn faced each other. Shye hurried out with waters and menus, giving all three of us quick hugs and welcoming smiles before hustling her way to other tables. No matter the activity in the restaurant, though, I couldn't help but watch the door. Every time that darn bell rang, I glanced up, expecting to see someone I knew. Someone I was waiting for without actually waiting for them. That totally didn't make sense, but I had a feeling—an intuition. My one-night stand was from Justice, and there was no way I would be avoiding him for this entire week home.

Ugh, I should have stayed in Denver.

The next time the bell rang and a group of men walked in, Elijah pushed his glass of water my way.

"Here," he said, giving me a sly smile when I looked his way. "You seem really...thirsty."

If I hadn't loved the man so much, I would have killed him. "I am not thirsty, you jackass. I'm just distracted. There're a lot of people coming in for lunch."

"Katie's is all there is in town," Finn said, smiling as Shye once again approached our table. "And the food is amazing. Every Justice resident and even a few from Rock Falls will be in over the next couple days."

"Hey, sorry," Shye said, looking frazzled. "We're really busy, but I didn't want you to think I'd forgotten about you. Have you decided on lunch?"

Once she had our orders noted, Shye disappeared into the crowds of people while we went back to small talk. Our food came quickly enough, and we set about eating, chatting, and waving to people we knew from growing up in town. Nothing too exciting, nothing out of the ordinary. I couldn't sit still, though. That feeling of impending doom, of knowing something was going to happen, only grew as I sat.

Finally, I'd had enough.

"I think it's time to go," I said, tossing my napkin over my plate and rising to my feet. "I really want to unpack then track down Mercy."

Elijah looked positively dumb struck. "Already?"

"Yeah, already."

"We have to say goodbye to Shye," Finn said, grabbing the last bite of his roll. "She can put the bill on my tab for us."

"You two finish up. I'll take care of that." I headed for the counter where Shye was pouring a few drinks, giving her a smile as I approached. "We're going to head out. Finn said to put the meal on his tab."

Shye shot me a knowing grin. "Yeah, like Katie will let me do that. Y'all go on, though. It was good to see you."

"You, too." I waited for a moment, trying really hard to figure out what to say to this woman I barely knew. The one who had somehow become a sister to me. "I'm looking forward to Thanksgiving. Thank you for inviting us."

"It's my pleasure. I'm looking forward to all of us being together without the crazy backdrop of a wedding getting in the way." She reached across the counter and grabbed my hand, giving it a squeeze. "It'll be nice to get to know you as my sister."

Yeah, that was...awkward and uncomfortable. I could be an adult, though.

"Absolutely. I'm sure we'll have some time this week."

"I hope so. Alder would love it if we got along."

I bristled. It was involuntary—the automatic stiffening whenever my eldest brother's name was mentioned. I struggled to smile back and nod when what I really wanted to do was interrogate her on what that meant. As if Alder thought I wouldn't get along with his wife? As if he thought I wouldn't at least try? The man's arrogance wasn't hers, though. So I bit back my retorts.

I was going to end up with a headache from holding my tongue.

I turned to leave, ready to head back to the apartment with the twins, when a man caught my attention. Two, really. Alder—brother of the attitude—stood in the doorway, staring my way. But it wasn't his formidable presence that struck me. It was the man next to him— the one who stood a little shorter. The one with the messy brown curls and green eyes that set my soul on fire. The man I'd secretly been waiting for. The one who'd fucked me and left me. The one who'd ignored me at Alder's wedding as if the night in my bed had never happened. The man I simply couldn't stop thinking about.

"Lainie?" Alder—eldest brother and bane of my existence— stuttered to a stop, looking as if I'd somehow taken him by surprise. "Well, what do you know. My baby sister's back in town."

My immediate response was to remind him that I was not a baby, but it seemed pointless because I couldn't look away from the man by his side.

Deacon Manns.

Giver of the best sex of my life.

The man there was no way I could have.

Because he was my eldest brother's best friend.

Happy Thanksgiving to me.

Chapter Three

DEACON

I couldn't look at her, but I couldn't look away either. Which made no sense, and yet, there I was. Looking and not looking. Checking out every inch possible without actually meeting her gaze. Trying my hardest not to end up being some sort of creeper.

But my God...the woman could wear a pair of jeans.

"Hey, Deacon," Alder said, knocking me hard with his elbow. "You remember Lainie, right?"

Remembered was an understatement. "Of course. Yeah."

"My baby sister—home for the holiday."

"I'm not a fucking baby," she said, the tone one that broke my need to not look. Our eyes met, and the fire there, the heat. My God, she was just so beautiful, and I was an absolute fool in every way for taking her when I shouldn't have and then walking away from her when I figured out who she was. A fool.

"Right, not a baby." Alder laughed, knocking me with his elbow again, which was really a damn annoyance. "Lainie sits on her phone all day and looks at her social media accounts instead of working, but she's not a baby."

Lainie's expression changed to one of pure rage, not that I blamed her.

"You're an idiot if you believe that nonsense." I really enjoyed putting Alder in his place when his head got too big; I did. But this was something else. This wasn't him being overly protective or intrusive—that comment was mean. And I wasn't going to stand for him cutting that woman down. "She's got a degree in communications with an emphasis on digital marketing, an MBA, and is about to get her master of arts in media and public communications. She doesn't just sit and stare at social media accounts—she strategizes social media content for businesses and sets them up to scale."

The world went silent, everyone turning to look at me as if I had just said something surprising. Which was ludicrous. Even before I'd met Lainie, I had known from Finn what her educational and work experiences were. The two youngest Kennard brothers were quite proud of their sister. Alder...well, he had a tendency to dismiss things he didn't understand, and social media happened to be one of those things. Obviously.

"Thanks for throwing up the shield," Lainie said, still glaring my way. "But I don't need a white knight to protect me. You ready to go, Elijah?"

Elijah and Finn appeared at her side, both of them looking a bit uncomfortable to be caught in the Lainie-versus-Alder show. Me? I was into it. I always did like putting Alder in his place, plus I really liked Lainie looking at me. Just looking. I shouldn't like that as much as I did, but what could I say? Daytime Deacon was as much of a bastard as nighttime Deacon, apparently.

"You don't have to leave just because I showed up," Alder said, crossing his arms over his chest. "You could stay so we can chat."

Lainie was shaking her head before he even finished that statement. "Elijah and I just made it into town. We stopped here for lunch but need to go unpack still. We'll have plenty of time to *chat*, big brother." She glanced my way again, a small smile tugging at those pink lips before she returned her gaze to Alder. "Besides, I need to track down Mercy to set up a girls' night out."

"The Jury Room is closed." My response came unbidden, my need to interject myself into her life almost instinctual. I should have known better. Lainie turned my way, a cruel, almost predatory expression on that beautiful face. That Kennard look. I'd just played into her hands, and she was going to exploit that weakness for all its worth.

"I'm not afraid to hit up the bars outside of town, Deacon. You, of all people, should know that."

My stomach sank, and a sudden cold sort of sweat broke out along my body. She was right—I should know that. I *did* know that. I'd met her at the Tracks in Rock Falls. I'd been at the bar enjoying an old-fashioned when that gorgeous creature had sat down beside me and ordered a chocolate martini. I hadn't recognized her, and when she'd introduced herself as Elaine, I'd had no reason to assume any sort of connection to her. No one called her Elaine in Justice—she was Lainie. But that night, she'd been Elaine.

And for the briefest of moments, she'd been mine.

I gave her a nod, bowing out as gracefully as possible. "I do, and I'm sure any smart business owner would be thrilled to have your face taking up residence at their bar."

She blinked, the anger fading for just a moment. The true her—the funny, smiling, amazing her—showing through. But then Alder moved as if to approach her, and she threw that wall right back up.

"Whatever. It's good to see you, brother." And with that, she strolled past the two of us. Elijah and Finn followed, pausing to shake hands with Alder and me.

Elijah even tossed out a *"Sorry, man"* to Alder, not that it mattered.

Once they were all gone, Alder took a deep breath and shook his head. "I will never know what I did to that girl to deserve such hatred."

"Maybe mocking her career choice. Just a thought."

He jerked my way, looking shocked. As if he didn't even realize how mean he had come off just a few minutes before. "I wasn't mocking her. I was only joking."

I didn't answer him, because at that moment, Shye came hustling into the dining room, and the man's focus deserted his sister and instead locked on to his wife.

Another day, another conversation. Another attempt to make Alder realize some things about his own behavior that might be hurting others.

Because Lainie didn't hate her brother. That much was obvious. She loved him very much. She also needed more from him than he'd ever been willing to give her.

Those harsh words and steely looks weren't given in anger. That was pure pain.

* * *

A man never really notices the number of blades, grinders, and machines that could easily kill and cut a body up into pieces until he felt as if he deserved a little torture and death for what he'd done. That thought could also be known as "the man who pulled a fuck and run on the mill owner's little sister walks through the mill."

"Let me just find Gage. He was supposed to pop in after lunch to work on a shredder." Alder stormed off, not tossing my ass into said broken shredder, for which I was grateful. I hadn't been able to stop thinking about Lainie since we'd left the restaurant. Hadn't been able to get our night with her as Elaine off my mind. Not just the dirty parts—I wasn't a complete perv—but the good parts, too. The chatting, the joking, the laughing. I hadn't known she was a Kennard then, hadn't even put together the Elaine-equals-Lainie thing and, frankly, hadn't asked her last name. Hadn't known simply giving in to the attraction between us and going back to her hotel would throw my life into such chaos.

I hadn't intended to fuck and run, see. Hadn't been in it for the one night. I would have followed that girl around like a puppy with my tongue hanging out, just hoping for a little more attention from her. She was everything a man could want—smart, sexy, witty, and way too much for me to handle. Dating up, the kids called it. As in, I was the lesser of the two, but I would have tried. I would have done my best to make her happy and keep those blue eyes focused on mine. I would have held on to her with both hands. But her last name was Kennard, and that had made letting her go the smarter decision.

Though I was beginning to question my definition of smarter.

Gage and Alder turned a corner, both looking pretty menacing in the shadowy mill. The place was closed, but this was where Alder felt comfortable talking Soul Suckers business. I didn't question it.

"How's it going?" Gage gave me an elbow bump, his hands obviously too dirty to be offered. I appreciated the consideration.

"S'all good, man. What's on the agenda?"

Alder leaned against some monstrous-looking metal thing that likely had teeth that could rip my flesh from my bones. "We need to be both on offense and defense this week. I want us in two teams to that end—one doing all the protection and surveillance, the other seeking out the Soul Suckers and setting up confrontations."

Yeah, that sounded smart. "It'll stretch us a little thin, but I can call in Zane to assist."

Gage nodded, crossing his heavy arms over his chest. "I want to lead up the defense. Bishop and I, really. He's not as dialed in as he needs to be to lead an attack."

Because of his wife—the woman he'd quietly married in Las Vegas—who was currently carrying their first child. Yeah, I couldn't blame him for that.

More kids were coming to Justice. Babies. Families...easy targets for those who wanted to hurt the men in town. We were going to need more guns.

"I'll get a supply order in," I said, my mind spinning in a hundred directions. "If there's anything specific you want, let me know. Otherwise, I'm going to order heavy, and we'll divvy up supplies."

"Get Bishop something that goes boom real good," Gage said, his thick beard ticking up on one side. A sure sign of a smile. "He's going to want a fucking rocket launcher on his porch once that baby arrives."

Alder chuckled, nodding. "You bet your ass he will. He's the protective sort by nature—he had poor Lainie encased in bubble wrap for a few years there."

And there it was—the connection. The reminder that I'd fucked up good. The link between Lainie and her older brothers, who were some of my best friends.

I really did deserve to be thrown in the shredder.

"We good, then?" I asked, unable and unwilling to hang out and shoot the shit. "I need to get back home."

Alder shook his head. "I've got some work to do still. You heading into town, Gage?"

The beast of a man nodded. "I got you, Deac. Let me just wash up, and I'll meet you at my truck."

I wasn't unhappy to get away from Alder, wasn't unhappy to walk out of the mill in one piece either. There was just one thing I couldn't let go of from my meeting with the two of them.

"Where's your sidekick?" I asked as Gage exited the mill and walked toward his truck, where I stood. "I haven't seen Rex all day."

Gage huffed, unlocking the doors and indicating I should hop inside. "He's still at the restaurant with Katie." He started the engine with a roar, giving it a little gas to warm it up before throwing the thing in reverse. "Damn mutt likes that girl more than he likes me."

Alder, Bishop, Gage, Finn—all whipped by the women who'd stormed into their lives. Even our friend Chase had been caught and tagged by a local. I was feeling extra single all of a sudden.

"Can't say I blame him," I said, watching the forest roll by as Gage raced toward town. "You are the lesser of the two in that relationship."

"Don't I know it."

* * *

I ended up heading back out to Main Street in the early evening, looking to grab something for dinner real quick. I'd been home and making calls all afternoon, had exhausted my voice and my brain. I just wanted some soup and some quiet.

The universe was apparently going to refuse me the latter.

I had my soup in hand, had my head down and my eyes on the keys in my hand, when someone bumped into me on the sidewalk in front of The Baker's Cottage. Someone I recognized.

Someone who was wearing tight as fuck leggings, a sports bra thing, and running shoes.

Someone sweaty.

Why did God hate me so?

"Hey," I said, completely rattled. "You okay?"

She cocked her head, pulling out an earbud and giving me the most quizzical look ever. "Of course I am. Are *you* okay?"

"Not at all."

Her lips turned up, that smile I remembered from the bar—the first one, the shy one, the welcoming one—settling in. "Big boss driving you crazy?"

Big boss. As in Alder. I took a step back, refocusing on my soup. "He's my best friend."

Her voice changed, her body language stiffening. "And more important to you than anything else."

Not true, but I didn't get the time to argue. Lainie took off at a jog again, literally running away from me as I stood there with my soup. As I readied myself to once again return home to an empty house and eat my meal alone.

As I regretted every single decision I'd made in my life that had led me to that moment.

Many hours and too much bourbon later, I sat in my recliner with my feet up in a dark and empty house. The ceiling was my entertainment, the memories playing in my mind like a movie. I was just drunk enough to let myself fall into the loneliness, just over the edge where my control could only whisper at me instead of scream.

I was just bored and relaxed enough to reach for my phone and do the thing I'd been wanting to do since Alder's wedding.

I'm sorry I'm an asshole. I'm sorry that things worked out the way they did.

Yeah, I had her number. Yeah, she'd texted me a handful of times, trying to find out why I'd run off and gone silent after our night together. And yeah, I needed to say a lot more than that to make up for how I'd treated her. But in the liquor-induced haze, that seemed like a good start.

It took more than a few minutes for her to respond, and when she did, I certainly didn't feel any better.

Your apology doesn't make this any easier.

Wasn't that the truth?

I pulled my sorry ass out of the chair and cleaned up, ready for bed, tired and cranky and all out of sorts. Memories of war and missions mixing with blond hair and soft skin as they played out in my mind simultaneously. My life had been tied to the Kennards for almost two decades, had been entwined with Alder's all that time. He'd taken a damned bullet for me—had almost died for me—and I still owed him for that. But at two in the morning after drinking almost half a bottle of rye whiskey and missing the soft, sweet touch of a particular woman, some cracks developed in my loyalty to the man.

Phones were the devil, text messages were his favorite tool, and I was not one to resist temptation when intoxicated.

I'm sorry I met Alder first.

What came back a minute later wasn't a message from Lainie, though. It was one from Alder himself.

Soul Suckers rolled down the highway about ten minutes ago. Chase saw them pulling out of the lot at your bar and called me. Want to check it out?

Motherfucker. Suddenly sober and really fucking glad I had finished my orders and plans earlier in the evening, before opening the whiskey, I tapped the alarm app on my phone and flipped to the camera feeds. Inside and outside looked quiet, and all the sensors were reading as secured. I tapped through the history, making sure no one had gotten inside, before reviewing the feed from the camera on the front door. In grainy black-and-white, I watched the bikers roll into the lot. They sat for only about a minute, lighting up the front of the motel at the back of the property. Engines grumbling loudly in the otherwise quiet night. Then, just as quickly and smoothly as they had arrived, they turned and left. Not one person even got off his ride.

Odd.

Once the last bike had rolled back onto the highway, I closed that app and swiped for my messenger one.

No need. They rolled in but never got off their bikes. The bar is secure.

Which felt weird. Why would they have shown up there? Why were they shining their lights on the motel—where no one had stayed since Chase had moved out in October—instead of the bar?

I didn't have an answer to those when my phone lit up again. This time, the message was from Lainie, and it was hurtfully direct.

Not good enough.

She was right. I wasn't good enough in a lot of ways. Especially when it came to her.

Alder sent the next message I received. A quick one saying *We need to make offensive plans in the morning,* which meant I needed to get some sleep. I sent him back a quick *Roger that* before typing one last message. One last text. Not for Alder this time. One last comment to his sister because I needed to say it.

Justice isn't as safe as it used to be. Be careful.

And with that, I tucked my phone beneath my pillow, slammed my head into the feathery softness, and tugged a blanket up around my shoulders. I needed to sleep off the liquor if I was going to be any good for the team. Just a few hours of rest would reset my brain and allow me to focus on the business at hand, which was keeping everyone in Justice safe. Not just Lainie.

Even if every plot and possibility for an upcoming battle centered on making sure she was the first one who got out alive.

Chapter Four

LAINIE

I'm sorry I met Alder first.

I woke up thinking about that text. Showered while thinking about that text. Stood in the bathroom putting on my makeup, thinking about that text. And for all the time I spent examining every syllable, I only had one response.

That was a bullshit text from a bullshit man.

A pounding on the bathroom door made me jump, and I dropped my hairbrush. "What?"

"How can it take you so long to get ready?" Elijah hollered through the door, giving it another pound for good measure. I huffed and retrieved my hairbrush from the floor, still thinking about that text. Unable not to.

I'm sorry I met Alder first.

"I'm sorry I ever met Deacon Manns at all," I grumbled to myself as I brushed out my hair.

Another knock on the door sounded. "If you don't open this door in two minutes, I'm coming in there."

I leaned over and reached for the doorknob, pulling open the door to the hallway to see a very irritated-looking Elijah. Irritated and...messy.

"What happened to your hair?"

My brother pushed the door open and barged inside, moving past me to turn on the spigot in the shower. "It's just bed head, hence the need for a shower."

Except I'd been living with Elijah for a few years at this point. I knew his bed head. This was not what I would have expected. *This* was sex hair.

"Did you have someone over last night?"

He brushed past me again, slipping into the hallway and throwing open the linen closet. "Of course not. Why would you think that?"

Because it looked like someone had been raking their fingers through his hair. "No reason, I guess. Just wondering why you look as if you've been ridden hard and put up wet."

He slammed the linen closet door closed, a towel in hand, and shoved his way past me. "I didn't sleep well. Are you done yet?"

I really hated dealing with cranky Elijah. "Not yet—I want to throw my hair into a bun really quick."

"Do it." He turned and tugged his shirt over his head, hooking his thumbs into the waistband of his shorts once the white fabric hit the floor. "You'd better hurry up. I'm not waiting on you."

"Ew, Elijah. I don't need to see my big brother naked."

He stepped into the shower, closing the curtain behind himself but continuing our conversation, albeit in a louder voice. "Pretty sure you've seen a naked man before. Unless you're going to try to play the whole virginal baby sister act for Alder."

My eyes rolled so hard of their own volition that I was pretty sure I saw stars. "Not hardly."

Especially not after I'd screwed Alder's best friend. Multiple times. Not that I was about to tell anyone that little secret.

I finished brushing my hair and flipped it into a messy bun, leaving Elijah to shower off whatever sins he'd dirtied himself with alone. There were more important things to me in that moment than trying to figure out what my brother was up to, the most pressing being finding a decent cup of coffee.

"My kingdom for an espresso machine."

I was about to tug on my sneakers so I could head over to The Baker's Cottage when a knock sounded on the door to the apartment. I opened it hesitantly, not sure who to expect.

Mercy stood in the hallway with a carafe of what smelled like coffee in her hands. "Morning, sunshine."

I swung the door wide, motioning her in. "That had better be what I think it is."

"Coffee. Strong, black coffee. It's not espresso, Miss Fancy Pants, but it will hold up to any sort of milk or sweetener you want." She tugged a Mason jar out of her pocket and set it on the counter. "I even brought half and half in case you didn't have any."

Bless her. "You are my new best friend."

Mercy huffed a laugh, heading for a cabinet and grabbing down a couple of mugs I hadn't even known were there. "Don't tell Katie that."

"Don't tell Katie what?" The woman herself strolled into the apartment with a bakery box in her hand. "You just got to town, and you're already keeping secrets?"

I nearly flinched as a picture of Deacon darted through my mind. "I was just telling Mercy she was my new best friend for bringing over coffee. Want some?"

Katie shook her head and set down the box. "No thanks. I'm wired enough in the mornings. Gage might rethink being with me if I got any more energized."

Mercy snorted, pouring a cup of coffee and handing it to me. "Not hardly. I'm pretty sure you could get away with just about anything where Gage is concerned. You've got that man wrapped."

Katie looked down, grinning and shrugging a shoulder. "Maybe."

Oh, that maybe spoke volumes. That maybe was a definite sign of more to come—things like white dresses and vows, like cribs and tiny socks. That maybe was a dream of forever finally in reach. I envied that maybe hard.

Katie snapped out of her daydream quick, though. Giving Mercy a sly smile. "I'm sure you wouldn't know anything about having a man wrapped, now would you, Mercy? I mean, there's just that big, burly Marine who happens to hang around you and Beckett an awful lot."

Mercy's eyebrows flew up, the most exaggerated shocked expression ever on her face. "Are you implying I have Chase wrapped around my finger?"

"Pinkie," I said, nodding as I took my first sip of go-go juice. "He needs to be wrapped around your *pinkie*."

"He is," said Katie with a grin. "He totally is."

"He who and is what?" Elijah appeared from the hallway, looking far more put together than he had before his shower. His hair was still damp and he was just tugging down his sweater, but he definitely made an impression. The two women both went silent for a moment, likely looking at Elijah the way most women did.

The man was handsome as hell and deserved the looks.

"We were just talking about how Katie and Mercy both have their men wrapped around their pinkies." I nodded toward the carafe and mug. "Mercy brought coffee."

"Yes, please." He grabbed the cup, shooting Mercy a wink. "Must be a lucky man to have caught your attention, Merc. Maybe I should be jealous."

I snorted a laugh, knowing way too much about my brother to let that comment pass by. "You've never been jealous of anyone."

He shrugged, giving the ladies a smirk. "She might be right, but things do change."

Katie chuckled and reached for her phone, checking the screen. "Hanging out with you three all day would be a blast, but I've got a restaurant to run and a boyfriend wondering where I went and if I need rescuing." She rolled her eyes in a good-natured sort of way, reaching to give me a quick hug. "It's good to see you. Stop by for lunch and to chat."

"Of course." I was walking her to the door when I stopped in midstep, remembering my annoying interaction with Deacon and Alder the day before. "We should do a night out...the three of us."

"Not me?" Elijah said, pouting. "That's just mean."

"Girls' night. We haven't had one in forever." I turned to Mercy. "Think you could find a babysitter?"

She shrugged. "Chase could watch Beckett for me."

That floored me. "You trust him with Beckett?"

Because Mercy was nothing if not protective. If she would let this new guy spend time alone with her son, things were serious. Maybe more serious than I'd realized.

Mercy got that same look Katie'd had, seemingly both happy and almost embarrassed. "Things are good with him. We're...happy."

Elijah caught my eye, raising a brow at me. "Looks like I'm far too late to be jealous. First, you were dating Finn, now Chase. I just keep missing my shots."

"Somehow I doubt you'd miss much of anything if you really didn't want to," Katie said, blowing a kiss his way and waving before heading for the door. "The menfolk around here are never going to let us out on our own with all the stuff that's been happening. We'll need a chaperone."

I nearly spat out my coffee. "A what?"

"A chaperone," Mercy said, not sounding the least bit insulted or surprised. "I know you're sort of aware of what's been happening in Justice, but I don't think you know the whole truth. It's bad, Lainie. Katie can't open the restaurant without someone guarding the street, and my hardware store is closed to shoppers without an appointment. The Soul Suckers—they're dangerous. They got a hold of Beckett and put a knife—"

She stopped, shaking her head once and taking a deep breath. Regaining her control, it seemed.

"I knew things were bad, but—"

"They're worse than bad," Katie said, her voice a little duller. A little quieter. "But we can still have fun. I'll ask Gage to come with us. He's totally cool about stuff and won't be intrusive."

"He can also scare the crap out of people with a simple look," Mercy said. "So yeah, we'll need a chaperone. Gage is a good one."

"I'll tell him. Got a day in mind?"

I shrugged, still stuck on the whole needing a chaperone thing. "Tuesday night? Wednesday?"

Mercy nodded, heading for the door to follow behind Katie. "We've promised Shye to come help prep cook on Wednesday, so maybe that night. We can drag her married butt out with us. Give your eldest brother an attack of the worrywarts."

Now *that* sounded like a fun idea. "Perfect. Let's do it."

"I'll talk to Gage." Katie spun as she entered the hallway, shooting Elijah a grin. "Behave yourself, Elijah Kennard, or I'll make Gage bring you along as backup."

Elijah shrugged, still sipping his coffee as he leaned against the kitchen counter. "That sounds like the perfect reason to misbehave if you ask me."

"And on that note," Mercy said with a laugh. "I need to go collect my men—the little one and the big one. I'll pop over later to check in on you, okay?"

I nodded, reaching for a hug. "Please do. I've missed you."

Mercy held on to my shoulders a little longer than usual, giving me an almost sad smile. "I've been here the whole time, Lainie. You just have to be willing to come home now and again."

And with that, she strolled out the door, leaving me with a little residual guilt for my avoiding Justice.

Just a little.

"You can come to girls' night if you want," I said, catching Elijah's eye. "It might be fun."

"I'll skip the estrogen fest, but thanks." He poured out the last of his coffee and rinsed the mug, setting it at a perfect angle next to the sink. "You should definitely go, though. Who knows—you might find yourself a man on the Front."

His words, while innocuous in intention, hit me like a sandbag to the gut. Find myself a man. Too bad that wasn't what I wanted.

See, I'd found the man; he just didn't care about me enough to be willing to fight for me.

I didn't need a new one.

I needed the one I'd picked to grow a pair.

Chapter Five

DEACON

A morning without your pretty smile shining my way is a wasted morning." I ran up onto Alder and Shye's porch, giving my best friend a wink as I sidled in close to drop a kiss on his wife's cheek. "How you doing there, lovely? This old goat treating you well?"

Shye giggled and clutched her coffee cup a little tighter, glancing at her husband for a second before coming back to me. "I'm good, Deacon. Can I get you some coffee?"

The woman was as sweet as they came, but I wasn't about to ask her to give up her rocking chair for something so trivial. "I'm good, but thank you. Maybe I'll grab a warmer for my travel mug before I go, though."

"We've got plenty." She moved as if to get up, but Alder shook his head.

"We do," Alder said, his long legs stretched out in front of him, his heels resting on the porch railing. "But he can get his own, honey."

I stepped back and leaned my hips against the railing, crossing my arms over my chest. "You ready for a day of plotting and planning?"

Alder took a sip of his coffee and nodded. "Just about. Shye here wanted to have coffee on the porch so we could enjoy the warmth before the snow started falling again."

Translation—he wasn't unassing that chair until his wife was good and ready for him to do so. Smart, smart man.

"You two should go," Shye said, tugging the blanket on her lap a little closer. "I'm going to head inside once I finish my coffee anyway."

Alder nodded and set down his cup, dropping his heels to the floor so he could rise to his feet too. "All right, then. We're just heading over to Bishop's to deal with a few things. Anabeth will be on her way here once I tell Bishop we're leaving. Rusty from the mill is on the property to keep an eye on things while I'm gone, but stay inside and lock up the house, okay?"

Shye laughed again, softer this time. Not nearly as convincing as her true giggle. "You're way too overprotective. Go on—I'll be just fine."

But Alder and I both knew her concept of *just fine* and ours were very different. We'd taken a weekend away to rid the world of the man who'd taught her that cruelness was normal, that threats and beatings were to be expected. I had no regrets for that kill because Alder's Shye was a woman of worth who deserved to understand *normal* meant so much more.

Alder, always one to be ready to spoil his woman, leaned over to give her a kiss goodbye. Unfortunately for me, this wasn't a quick peck. Oh no, Alder laid it on thick, kissing her deeply and even adding in a little moan at the end. I snuck away and slipped inside, travel mug in hand, eyes locked on their coffee machine. I could give them a minute to get that kiss out of their system and grab a little more coffee to keep my morning running. Win-win, really.

Mug refilled, eyes hopeful that I wouldn't need to see Alder still stuck to Shye's face, I crept back onto the porch. The two lovebirds were thankfully only hugging at that point. Good.

"All ready," I said, giving them both a grin. "Thanks for the coffee, Shye. A man could get used to being spoiled by you."

"Anything for Alder and his friends." She tucked her head against Alder's chest, looking truly happy in that moment. Jealousy reared its ugly head inside me, the nothingness of my life scraping at my guts. Not nothing, I had to remind myself. Just mine and not shared.

Still a sucky place to be.

"I'll be home later. Text me if you need anything." With that, Alder gave Shye one last quick kiss on the top of her head then turned and headed for my truck, both of us quiet until we had hopped inside and closed the doors.

"She'll be safe out here?"

Alder nodded, tugging his phone from his pocket. "I wasn't kidding about Rusty. I just didn't let her know that I've got two other guys on the outskirts of the property and Barney the mailman down on the road to keep an eye out while I'm off with you."

Because the man knew the threat would be focused on him, which meant Shye. The woman who had already paid enough of a price to the Soul Suckers. "Good. Someone following Anabeth over?"

Alder nodded, typing on the screen. "Yup. Bishop's got that covered. We should be good for a couple hours."

Should be wasn't good enough, though. Even I knew that. "We'll get this done as quickly as possible."

We made it to Bishop's without issue, passing Anabeth on the highway. We also passed Hunter, one of Gage's mechanics at the mill and the man who was apparently making sure Anabeth made it to Alder's house.

"What's up, brother?" Bishop asked, meeting us on the porch of what was old Miss Hansen's place but now belonged to her granddaughter, Anabeth Kennard. Wife of Bishop and soon-to-be mother of the first of the next Kennard generation. Another lucky SOB. Today was truly not my day to be around these paired-off men.

I'm sorry I met Alder first.

Fuck me, it was going to take a long time to get that thought out of my head.

"Let's get to work," Bishop said, leading the two of us inside. "Gage wants to get back downtown as soon as possible."

Because his girl Katie would be working down there at her restaurant. Seriously, this was not the day to be around these men.

We headed inside and set up around the living room, Gage looking edgy and menacing in the corner, while Bishop and Alder took opposite ends of the couch. I settled myself in a wingback chair.

"This your usual spot?" I gave Bishop a head nod, rubbing the arm of the flower-covered arm. "You like this chair for watching the games on Sunday?"

Bishop huffed a laugh and shook his head. "We've still got a lot of Miss Hansen's stuff to deal with and plans for remodeling, but it's hard on Anabeth. She's still grieving, you know?"

I did know. Losing the person she had seen as a mother must have been brutal for Anabeth. That was why she had come back to Justice in the first place—to say goodbye and usher her grandmother into her next adventure. No one had expected her to stick around. Least of all Bishop.

Thank fuck we'd all been wrong because the man seemed really fucking happy.

"I'm just busting your balls," I said in way of apology. Not that I needed one—Bishop wasn't an easy man to offend.

"So, what's the plan?" Gage asked, redirecting us back to the subject at hand. "How are we going to handle this new threat?"

Alder sat forward, resting his elbows on his knees as he looked at each of us in turn. "It's time to take them all out."

"We initiate?" I asked, because we tended to stick to defensive tactics.

"If they're in Justice, they're a threat," Alder replied, not budging off his idea. "We clean house."

Which meant killing each and every one of them. Murder without cause wasn't ever my first choice, but Alder seemed set. We would all follow his lead.

As Alder began talking about search parties and hunting out the Soul Suckers' camp, my phone buzzed. I tugged it out of my pocket and read the message, unease turning my stomach a little.

"Zane texted," I said, still staring at the screen. "The sheriff's office is aware that there are Soul Suckers in the area and are asking their officers to keep an eye on Justice."

Gage whistled. "That's some prophetic timing right there."

"But does it change our plans?" I asked, eyeing Alder. "Because no one wants to see a man go to jail."

"True." Alder sat back, rubbing his forehead for a second. "We just need to keep things clean. If there're no bodies, there're no cases. If there's no proof we were around, there're no charges."

Bishop coughed, looking mighty uncomfortable. I understood his hesitancy—he had a wife and a baby on the way. Prison wasn't in his plans. Gage would follow whatever Bishop did, which meant we could have two men down if we played this wrong. And Alder wasn't one to be as sensitive to the moods of his men as he should have been.

Time to take a little control. "So, we slow our roll a little. We can still take out the Soul Suckers, but we need to be more reserved about it. Stealthier. Sniper action instead of kicking down doors."

Bishop nodded. "Yeah. This is definitely more your realm than ours."

Because as a sniper for the Army Special Forces, my training was quieter than theirs. Bishop and Gage had been SEALs—lots of brash. Lots of showboating. We were the subtler ones.

We were also sneaky as fuck. "We're going to need a scapegoat, too."

Alder didn't look pleased. "Where are we going to find someone who deserves that level of blowback thrown at them?"

Gage took that one. "The Black Angels were pretty much decimated by the Soul Suckers just recently. Seems to me we've got one if we report a few sightings of them in the area."

Damn, the man had brains. I sat back in my floral throne, grinning at a slightly unhappy Alder. "Zane can help us there as well. We should ask Elijah for his assistance, too."

"No," Alder said, not even giving the idea time to filter through. "Why would you want Elijah involved?"

"Because he's fucking smart. He's a lawyer, so he thinks differently than we do and can help us keep our profile low."

"I don't like it," Alder said.

Bishop was the one to argue with his brother this time, though. "I do. Elijah's an attorney—he knows the stuff that happens beyond the arrest and the charges filed. We need his expertise just in case something goes wrong."

"What else?" Gage asked, looking more and more like a caged animal as time passed. "What more do we need to worry about today?"

"Weapons," I said. "I've already got an order out to stock up. Other than that, we just need to make sure Zane and Elijah are on board, then we're ready to plan out phase two."

"What about Finn?" Bishop asked, looking toward his brother. "Jinx, too."

"Keep them out of it." Alder rose to his feet, pacing. "In fact, we should send them out of town. We don't need the liability of the two of them hanging around."

Finn was not going to like that idea. But it wasn't the third Kennard brother I was focused on in that moment. It was the second. Bishop looked agitated, his leg bouncing and his teeth biting into his lip. I'd never seen him so nervous.

Obviously, neither had Gage. "She's safest with you."

Bishop shook his head, still fidgeting. "It's not just her anymore, you know?"

Yeah, I did know. Bishop's load had doubled when Anabeth had announced she was pregnant.

"Keep her with you," I said. "Keep her at your side as much as possible. When you can't, we've got your back."

Bishop nodded, still looking uncomfortable. We'd need to make the same promise to Chase if we were going to ask him to help, which we would. Chase didn't have a pregnant bride—he had a little boy to worry about. Mercy and Beckett may have only recently come screaming into his life, but that didn't matter. He'd die for them. Something that definitely needed to be considered.

We wrapped up quickly, each man seeming to want to get back home. I mean, not me. Not really. I didn't have anyone waiting on me. I did wonder what Lainie was up to, but that was a thought path I needed to avoid. At least until I was out of sight of the Kennard men.

But thoughts of the fairest Kennard invaded my mind once again as Alder and I loaded into my truck. Of what I would do if someone got their hands on her. Of the danger of having a single woman alone in Justice right now.

Of what I needed to do to keep her safe.

"Thought about what to do with Lainie yet?" I asked, knowing Alder well enough to believe he had.

I wasn't wrong.

"We need to get Lainie out of town too," he said, no uncertainty evidenced in his voice. "She's a liability both as a single woman and as someone who doesn't and shouldn't understand what's happening here."

I threw the truck into gear, both relieved and anxious. I had a feeling being kicked out of town wouldn't go over well with the woman. I also had a feeling this decision would tie me in two. On the one hand, I wanted her in town. Selfish, yes. Slightly sadistic, seeing as how I couldn't do anything with her, absolutely. Didn't change the fact. On the other hand, I knew the very thought of her being in danger would drive me insane.

It was a lose-lose situation.

All for someone I really shouldn't have given so much thought to.

Fuck, I was going to regret the next thing out of my mouth no matter whether I agreed or disagreed.

Sorry, Lainie. It's for your own good.

"Let's make it happen."

Chapter Six

LAINIE

Saturday nights were supposed to be date nights in my world—both Elijah and I would find friends or someone to spend some time with, hit the town, and not worry about when the other came home. The agreement had worked out well for a number of years.

And then we came home to Justice.

"Bastard," I said around my spoon of cookie dough ice cream. "Leaving me home alone on a Saturday night is just cruel."

Fine, not cruel. And not Elijah's fault, really. He and Finn had wanted to do some *twin stuff,* as I'd always called it, which left me alone. And bored. And eating more ice cream than I should have. And wondering how long it would take for me to regret the decision to even open the carton.

I could have gone with Elijah—he'd invited me more than once—but that hadn't felt right. Neither did sitting home, though. Not that this borrowed apartment was really home. Justice hadn't felt like home to me in a number of years. Instead, it felt like that one sweater someone you cared about bought for you, the really nice one that never quite fit well. Being back in Justice made me feel as if I had that sweater on with the uncomfortable neckline and the sleeves that hugged a little too much and ended a little too far from my wrists. Being around friends and family almost made wearing that sweater worth the aggravation, until one of my brothers tried to tell me what to do or shoved me aside because I didn't happen to have a penis like the rest of them. Then that sweater became unbearable again, and I longed to go back to Denver and toss it into a drawer to be forgotten about for another six months. Back to the place that had never been home but was somehow better than Justice.

"You really need to get out more," I said to myself, irritated with the way my thoughts had turned. My skin practically itched with a need for *something* to do, and yet I sat. And I ate. And I watched really bad reality television and tried not to let my mind wander too deep into my issues with Justice.

I was halfway through the latest show—something about people getting out of prison and hooking up with those who had been talking to them while inside—when a knock sounded on the door. I jumped up, rushing toward the wood slab. *People. Fun. Excitement.*

But when I swung that door open, there were no people. Just a single man with a hangdog expression on his handsome face.

"Deacon." I leaned against the jamb, not minding a bit when my giant sweatshirt with no real semblance of a collar fell from my shoulder and exposed a little more skin than my shirts usually allowed. "Something I can do for you?"

Those green eyes locked on mine, a fire burning in them that made my heart beat a little faster.

"I'm sorry to bother you, but I saw the light on and thought I'd stop. I'm looking for Elijah."

I had the urge to tell him Elijah wasn't home and slam the door in his face, but his excuse didn't hold water. We had these things called cell phones—if he wanted Elijah, he could have called, texted, snapped, or WhatsApped the man. Who popped in instead of clicking on a screen a few times? He may have said he was there for Elijah, but that was a lie. One I was happy to ignore.

"He's not here, but you can come in if you want." I turned and walked back inside the apartment, half wishing he'd follow. Half wishing he wouldn't.

He did. Slowly and with much more reservation than I would have thought. "You...uh...doing okay here? Got everything you need?"

I settled on the couch, smiling a little at his obvious discomfort. "I'm good, yeah. Are you? You seem awfully uncomfortable."

He made a sound like a grunt, glancing around the room. Just... standing there in the entry to the living area as if he hadn't been invited.

"You can sit, you know." I patted the other end of the couch. "I won't bite."

That gaze jerked my way, those eyes pinning me in place. Yeah, the whole not-biting thing was a lie. I'd bitten him plenty the night we'd spent together. Every time he'd made me come—and there had been plenty—I'd found myself with my teeth in his flesh as I fought the urge to scream in pleasure.

Not the time for that memory, Elaine.

"I don't want to intrude," Deacon said, inching toward the couch. "Like I said, I was looking for Elijah. But you're good here alone? Feel safe?"

"Of course."

"Good. That's good. You've got enough food and whatever else you need, right? I can run into Rock Falls for you if there's something you want."

"Deacon, why are you—"

"How long are you staying?"

And there it was. That uncomfortable sweater was back on, making me feel as if I were choking. "Why?"

Deacon shrugged, still looking way too uncomfortable. "Alder and I were talking, and there are some plans we need to enact—"

"Hold on." I rose from the couch, my skin tight and burning but no longer from feeling uncomfortable. "Is that what this little visit is about? You came to see how long I would be a liability? What, did Alder not have the balls to ask me himself? Are you here to convince me to leave town and get out of the way?"

A tic started in his jaw, but he said nothing.

Nothing.

"Oh." I stopped, ending the pacing I hadn't even realized I had been doing right in front of the man. "I'm just an obstacle to your plans. I don't know why that surprises me—I've always been in the way where Alder is concerned."

Deacon shook his head slowly, keeping his eyes on mine. "You're not in the way, Lainie."

I hated when he used that nickname. "Don't lie to me."

"You're not in the way, but there are dangerous things in Justice these days. Alder and I—we don't want you getting near them." He stared me down, his voice dropping a bit as he said, "Or them getting anywhere near you."

There was so much more to unpack there, so much he was not

saying as he spoke those words. The tone, the grit in his voice—I was missing part of the story. "Why not?"

"Because we don't want you hurt."

We, we, we. He and Alder, yet my brother wasn't the one standing in the living room in front of me. "*You* don't want me hurt. Not we, you."

He held my gaze, that jaw clenched tight. "Fine. I don't want you hurt."

"Which is sort of surprising, Deacon." I stepped closer, invading his space. Refusing to back down. "Because you hurt me. Walking away the way you did and then ignoring me, acting as if we'd never met. That hurt."

He sighed, sagging as if surrendering to the weight he carried. "Lainie, I—"

"I hate it when you call me Lainie. My name's Elaine, and you know that."

His expression changed—his posture, too. The soldier appeared from where the uncomfortable man had stood, his eyes locking on me in a way that made the hair on the back of my neck stand up, his shoulders pulling back almost of their own volition. An unconscious sort of shift and one that made my heart beat a little faster. That confidence, that eagle-eyed stare—I remembered that energy from the night we had spent together. Remembered feeling as if he were hunting me.

"Don't tell me you don't remember," I said, shuffling an inch closer.

He matched my move, closing the gap between us an almost imperceptible amount. "Damn right, I remember."

"You disappeared on me."

"I figured out who you were."

"And then you avoided me at the wedding."

Another step closer, his arm brushing against mine. "You looked so damn beautiful that day."

"You noticed?" My voice didn't sound like it should—too breathy, too soft.

"Of course I noticed. I couldn't stop noticing." He broke the mood, taking a step back. Putting space between us once more. "But it was Alder's wedding, and you're his little sister."

That line punched me square in the gut. "Little nothing. I'm a full-grown woman."

"I'm aware."

"But you still see me as somehow belonging to Alder. As if my worth is tied to my relationship to him."

He frowned, that brow furrowing deep. "No. Not belonging. Just...connected."

I reclaimed the space between us, closing the gap once more. Refusing to make his escape easy. "I'm connected to you too."

Deacon sighed. "Lainie—"

"It's Elaine."

His countenance changed again, the soldier back and on the attack. He grabbed me by the shoulders and spun me around, herding me backward until he had me pinned against the wall. Until he had me entirely wrapped up in his scent, his heat, and his body touching mine. He was all I could see, all I could feel. And my goodness, did I like it.

"Deacon, I—"

"You don't get to be Elaine with me."

It was my turn to frown. "What?"

"If I call you Elaine—if I even *think* of you as her—tonight's going to be a repeat of last time. So no, Lainie, you don't get to be Elaine with me."

Which meant he wanted more. Which meant all these weeks of silence were because of Alder and not me. Which meant Deacon wouldn't choose me over my brother.

Typical.

"Pity," I said, pushing on his shoulder. "I think it's time for you to leave, then."

Deacon froze, once again shifting his body language and expression. Softening. I pushed again as a reminder of my demand, and he surrendered. Backing up and heading toward the door slowly, almost looking shaky.

Finally, he huffed and turned to look my way again. "This didn't go the way I'd planned."

"You mean you'd planned to come here and talk to me? You weren't looking for Elijah?" I took two steps closer, keeping distance between us but not giving up ground. "Do you ever tell the truth, Deacon? Even to yourself?"

He stood a little taller, glared a little hotter. "Here's the truth, Lainie. You're the sexiest woman I've ever seen, and that night with you haunts me every fucking day. But I'm old, and I'm set in ways you probably know nothing about. And the man who trusts me most in the world—to whom I owe my life five times over—is quite protective of you."

"So?"

"So, this casual shit you seem to want to play at can't happen. I won't disrespect the Kennards that way."

"What if it's more than casual?"

He was on me again in a second, his hands on my hips and his big body crowding mine against the counter. "You'd have to have my ring on your finger and be wearing my last name for Alder to be okay with us being together."

My heart skipped a beat, whether in fear or anticipation, I didn't know. But when I opened my mouth, it wasn't a refusal that came out.

"You offering?"

Deacon froze, blinking twice before he cocked his head and leaned over me. "You accepting?"

Pulse racing, joke no longer funny, I did my best to shrug in a casual manner even though I felt anything but casual. "I do like to piss off my brother now and again."

Deacon laughed, dropping his head to my shoulder and kneading the flesh of my hips where his hands still held me. "Woman, you're going to get me killed."

"Doubtful."

He rose to his full height, sighing again. That hangdog expression back. "He's likely to kick my ass from here to Wednesday just to prove the point that I never should have looked your way in the first place."

"You're afraid of him."

"No, I'm afraid of disappointing him."

That was almost worse. "He's not God."

"Never claimed he was." Deacon leaned closer again, breathing deep. Making me shiver as he whispered, "Go home, Lainie. Fuck Thanksgiving. Sunday morning—pack it up and head back to Denver where you'll be safe."

I clutched at his arms, wanting so much to surrender to him. To take him with me. To rescue him from being stuck in Justice under Alder's control. "Safe from what, Deacon? What are you trying to keep me away from?"

Deacon leaned down and placed the sweetest, softest kiss against my lips. It was almost unreal, too quick to sink into, too soft to be much more than a whisper.

"Everything," he said before he pulled away, heading for the door with a gait that ate up the floor. He was at the door in three beats, through it in another one. He gave me one last look, one final bask in that green gaze before he said, "I want you safe from everything, Lainie. Even me."

And then he was gone.

Chapter Seven

DEACON

Spending my morning with Alder after fighting with myself all night to not go back and crawl in between the legs of his little sister was a particular sort of torture I had not been prepared for.

"Hang on." Alder spun the wheel of his truck, hitting the dirt logger road a little harder and faster than most people would have. I did as I was told, reaching up to grab the oh-shit handle so I didn't get shaken up like a cocktail. "Sorry about that."

He wasn't sorry, not really. He was distracted, though. And fidgety.

"You okay over there?"

Alder sighed, tapping his fingers on the steering wheel as he drove us deeper into the forest. "I know they're coming."

They being the Soul Suckers, and yeah, they likely were. Hence the early morning drive to see if we could find a sign of where they were camping out. The weather had turned unseasonably warm

59

lately, the snow no longer falling. It was warm enough to stay outside and not suffer horribly—a fact not working in our favor.

For the first time in my life, I wished we were having ice storms and blizzards.

"They probably are coming," I said, knowing there was nothing I could do about the weather.

"There's no probably in my head," he said, risking a quick glance my way. "They'll wait for us to be distracted by the holiday, and then..."

He didn't need to get specific. "So, we don't get distracted."

"Easier said than done. Between Shye and the pressure she's putting on herself over this meal—"

"*She's* putting? You sure you're not heaping a little on her yourself?"

"Of course not. I told her we could have pizza for all I cared, but she's out to prove something. She wants the traditional spread with lots of sides and a perfect turkey. The woman's even making cranberry sauce from scratch. I actually like the canned stuff, but she's got it in her head that she needs to do all this extra shit."

"There won't be any canned cranberry sauce?"

"That's what I'm telling you."

"That's crazy." I huffed, slouching in my seat. "Does she realize we've spent years eating frozen turkey dinners or skipping that meal altogether and eating pizza or wings while watching football? We don't need fancy."

"Trust me, I keep telling her that." He shook his head, eyes on the road in front of him. "She's out to prove something that doesn't need proving."

That right there sounded like Shye for sure. "So, what do we do? How do we make this easier on her?"

He shrugged as we came to the end of the rut-filled stretch of land he called a road before swinging the truck around in a wide circle to go back the way we'd come. "Just eat it. Whatever she puts down, eat it. Praise her. I'm real fucking worried what she's going to do if something doesn't come out right."

"She's a good cook, though."

"A great one, but this is different for some reason. It's like she's trying to show everyone something, and I can't figure out what or how to help her."

"Well, you can count on me. I don't care if that bird is dry as a bone and the sides are all burned. I'll take one for the team." I smacked him on the arm, already chuckling. "Lord knows we've eaten worse."

"True facts, brother."

Alder got us back on the road and headed up into the mountains more, looking for old logging paths or anywhere a group of men could set up a camp of some sort. I had my doubts that the Soul Suckers would be solely on their motorcycles—good weather or not, being on a bike in late November in the mountains was a stupid decision—but Alder was convinced he needed to be looking for evidence of bikes. So, we drove and we looked and the man tried to kill me a time or two as he whipped that truck around in the woods he knew so well.

Meanwhile, I stewed on the plans and what was coming for us. "When are Finn and Jinx heading out of town?"

Alder grunted, looking to his left before making a right-hand turn. "First thing Friday morning. I wanted them to skip Thanksgiving dinner, but Finn refused. He's worried about Shye taking on too much as well, so Jinx is coming over to help her do prep and stuff."

"And they're heading to Denver?"

"Yeah—a long weekend in the city. I rented them a condo right on Sixteenth."

Tourist central. "Good call. I'll tell him about a couple places I've been to, make sure he can focus on having a fun experience and not the drinking and drug scenes."

"Thanks. I'm sure Jinx will keep him in line—"

"That woman would knock him on his ass if he even thought about messing up his sobriety."

Because Finn Kennard was an addict who'd spent a few years in prison for selling, even though he'd never sold so much as a dime bag. And Jinx...well, Jinx could hold her own. Alder and I had rescued her after dealing with Shye's stepbrother, a man who had beaten both women. Whipped them. We'd gone to take the man out of the equation of Shye's life and had come back with Jinx. Gift with purchase, so to speak.

She and Finn—well, they were two peas in a pod. Their attraction had been instant, and they were really good for each other. I'd seen it myself, how much she cared for the skinny Kennard. How she worried about and supported him. Those two were a good match, and no way would she allow Finn to risk his future.

One couple accounted for.

"Who else?" I asked, knowing Alder wouldn't stop there. "You sending Mercy and Beckett away too?"

"Chase is handling them. He doesn't want me involved, so I'm respecting his wishes."

Shocking. "So, that's it. Done."

Alder hemmed and hawed for a minute, something I knew meant the man had more to say. I waited him out, let him pull his thoughts together. He'd been my best friend for almost twenty years —I knew how to give him enough rope to hang himself.

And hang himself, he did. "I'm going to ask Anabeth to take Bishop and head back to Vegas for a few weeks."

There it was. "We all talked about this. Bishop was going to stay."

"I know that's what he said, but he seemed nervous. I don't want him distracted in a firefight."

"You think he doesn't know how to focus on the job?"

"I think the man is going to be a father, and that knowledge will weigh heavy on him no matter what situation he's in. He may not want to leave us to handle this shit, but he needs to go."

I didn't agree—not totally—but the desire to argue flew right out the window when I noticed a little disturbance in the sandy dirt on the side of the road.

"Those look like motorcycle tracks to you?"

Alder slammed on the brakes, leaning forward to get a better look. "Sure does."

I kept my eyes on the patches as Alder let the truck creep forward. "Could be dirt bikes."

"Could be Soul Suckers. Won't know until we find them."

"We're not armed enough to take on a club right now." Which wasn't even close to a lie. I'd brought a handgun and Alder had a shotgun in the cab with us, but that wouldn't be anywhere close to enough if we ran up on a full crew.

"We'll just take a look. We can always come back later with more supplies."

He turned onto another logging road, following the tread marks in the dirt. They didn't look all that new to me, didn't look fresh. It actually looked more like bikes had rolled through on a day when there had been rain or snow falling and the mud had eventually hardened with their tracks in it. Like a fossil, only not nearly as cool.

When Alder turned as if to follow a path deeper into the forest, I put a hand on his arm. "This is enough. Let's break out my new toy and let it do the work."

"They could be up there."

"Exactly. We aren't armed for that. This is supposed to be a surveillance run."

He chewed on his lip but eventually conceded, shutting off the engine and hopping out of the truck. I did the same, reaching into the bed for a box I'd secured there when Alder had picked me up. In it sat a very expensive, very cool toy I'd been dying to play with.

"How's this drone thing work anyway?"

I fired up the tablet that had come with it and linked it to my cell phone for data then headed to the clearing ahead of the truck to set things up.

"It has a camera. I input coordinates here, tell it what I want it to do—in this case, fly high and get a broad view of the forest—and we watch this tablet to see what it sees."

Alder didn't seem convinced, but he let me do my thing, which was good because as soon as that drone got in the air, we spotted more of the tracks leading into the forest.

"They went deep," Alder said, looking over my shoulder. "They didn't want to be spotted by anyone."

Truth. The tracks led farther into the forest than I'd have guessed, following an overgrown logging road that had definitely seen better days. The road ended at a wide clearing, an almost perfect circle with a rocky outcropping on one side.

"That spot's defensible as hell," I said, automatically figuring the best places to set up guards and snipers. "Someone knew what they were doing."

"Yeah, and definitely past tense. There's nothing there."

He was right about that—the clearing looked as if it had been empty for a while. Lots of tracks, a couple darkened spots that could have been fire pits, but nothing else.

Alder huffed and walked away, pacing. "Where the fuck could they be, and why were they up here in the first place?"

"Don't know, but I have a feeling we're going to find out." Eventually. Maybe this week. Maybe over the holiday. Maybe not until December. But my gut was telling me something was coming, something big. And we needed to be ready for it.

"Let's head back," I said, recalling the drone so I could pack everything up. "I've got a feeling these fuckers switched to cars when the first snow fell, which means their options are a bit more limited."

"What do you suggest we do?"

"I say we bust out the maps, head out tonight after dark, and let the drone do the surveillance for us."

"After dark?"

I grinned, guiding my drone into a near-perfect landing. "It's got night vision."

Alder whistled low. "Nice toy. Okay, Willy Wonka. We wait and follow your plan."

"Willy Wonka was candy, not toys."

"He had a fun house."

"It was a candy factory."

"Are you sure?"

As if. "Positive. The little boy in the chocolate river? The golden geese? Veruca Salt and Mike Teavee." I rose to my feet, my eyebrows lifting as I caught the blank stare on his face. "Have you never seen Willy Wonka?"

"I thought I had, but nothing you've just said is making sense to me."

I stormed up to him, making sure to get right in his face. "We are the music makers, and we are the dreamers of dreams."

His frown was deep and solid. Unchanging. "What the fuck are you talking about?"

"That's it. Text Shye and tell her I'm coming over. We're watching the fucking movie."

The man may have been my best friend in the world, but there were times I wondered what had gone wrong with him along the way. Never seen Willy Wonka?

I had work to do.

Chapter Eight

LAINIE

I hadn't planned on being at Alder's house on a Sunday night, I hadn't intended to show up and spend time with his new wife, but Shye had called. That was it. She'd called and asked me to come over. Somehow saying no to that had left me feeling guilty and bad, so I'd gone.

"She's a sorceress," I hissed at Elijah, who had also been somehow convinced with little more than a few words to show up at Alder's house. We were helping Shye move turkeys from their freezer into a bathtub. Something about them needing to thaw even though Thanksgiving was still four days away. Bathing the birds. That was our job.

Elijah nodded and set the big block of frozen bird in the tub next to mine. "A witch. Convincing us to come here to work without the promise of liquor or some other sinful reward is pure witchcraft."

"Agreed." I pasted a smile on my face and headed out into the living area. "Turkeys are bathing."

Shye—all ninety pounds of her—grinned my way, that smile lighting up the entire room. Like, almost literally. "Perfect. Thank you so much for carrying all of those. I would have waited for Alder, but I know he's been working all day."

I nodded, leaning closer to Elijah to whisper, "I thought the mill was closed."

"It is."

"So what has he been doing all day?"

"Not carrying turkeys."

Shocking. "See? It's witchcraft."

"You won't hear me arguing." He strode toward the open kitchen, raising his voice once more to address our sister-in-law. "What else can we do for you, Shye?"

She looked around the kitchen, biting her lip. "I don't think there's anything. Can I make you a coffee or something? Are you hungry? Oh! I have an icebox pie in the garage refrigerator. I'd been wanting to test the recipe, so I made one early. Let me get you some."

Elijah glanced my way, eyebrow curved up in question, as she hurried out the door. "You in?"

I shrugged. "Who turns down icebox pie?"

"Do I even know what icebox pie is?"

"Sort of like that lemon cheesecake thing I make."

He nodded. "Then we're staying."

The man was not one to turn down sweets.

Shye strolled back into the house carrying a pie and being followed by none other than my brother. "Look who just got home."

"Yeah, look." I jumped when Elijah elbowed me, pasting that smile back on my face. "Hi, Alder."

"Hey there, Lainie girl." He followed Shye to the counter, dropping a kiss on her neck and—dear god—giving her ass a smack. "Give me five to wash up, then I'll be here to help."

"Don't worry about it," Shye said, looking our way. "Elijah and Lainie helped with the turkeys. We're all done and about to enjoy some pie. Want me to make you a coffee?"

"That would be great, honey. Thank you."

And with that, he rushed up the stairs, disappearing just as the garage door opened again and none other than Deacon came strolling inside.

"Honey, I'm home." His grin faltered a bit when his eyes locked on mine, returning with a bright blaze as he obviously got over his surprise. "Two beautiful women in one house. Whatever did I do to deserve such a gift?"

"I'm not your gift, Deacon." Shye tossed a kitchen towel at him. "Did you wash your hands?"

"Yes, ma'am. And I left my boots in the garage." He pointed down at his socked feet. "I'm about as clean as you're going to get me."

So many jokes to be made about that statement, but so little time.

"You and Alder get some solid work in?" Elijah asked, the tone in his voice making me think he had known all along where Alder had been and simply hadn't told me. The bastard.

"Sure did. Flew the drone around for a few hours. Didn't spot anything out of the ordinary, but at least we knocked a few hiding places off the list of possibilities."

"Hiding places for what?" I asked.

Both men stopped to look at me, neither speaking.

I turned my gaze to Shye. "Is this how it always is around here?

The men refusing to tell the women what's happening?"

She shrugged. "Pretty much."

My eye roll physically hurt my head. "You're ridiculous, Deacon Manns."

He froze, not saying a word. Staring at me for a couple long and slightly awkward seconds. Then he cocked his head.

"We were looking for evidence of a group of the Soul Suckers motorcycle club being in town, Lainie."

I didn't know how to take that, what to do with having the truth laid out right there in front of me. Thankfully, Alder chose that moment to come pounding down the stairs.

"All right. Let's have some pie."

Don't ever let it be said that Alder Kennard didn't have a way with words.

As the evening progressed, pie was definitely eaten. We were also joined by Finn and his girlfriend, Jinx. If Bishop had been there, it would have been a full-on family reunion, but we capped out at the seven of us. Luckily, there was enough pie to go around.

"Shye, that was amazing," Deacon said as he brought his plate to the sink. He even dropped a little kiss on Shye's cheek. "Don't forget, I'm available as backup should that one over there let you down."

A flicker of jealousy lit up my chest even though I knew it was completely illogical to feel. One, Shye was madly in love with my brother. That was obvious. Two, Deacon would never stand against my brother, something I knew all too well. Three, my brother would kill that man if he even thought for a second Deacon was serious, best friend or no.

I sat a little deeper when Alder rose to his feet and started clearing the table. He even brought the coffeepot over to refill everyone's cups while Shye finished her own slice of dessert.

Deacon happened to have claimed the seat beside me, so I leaned toward him and lowered my voice. "Since when did Alder become a grown-up?"

"What do you mean?" Deacon said, zeroing in on my brother. "Oh, cleaning up? Shye cooks, he cleans. That's their deal."

I blinked, unable to believe my own eyes. "That never would have happened growing up."

He shrugged. "Men do eventually become adults."

"Only some."

"Very true."

I shook my head as Alder started hand-washing the dishes at the sink. "Witchcraft."

"You think Shye's a witch?"

"How else do you explain this magic?"

He took a moment to glance around the room, seeming to really take in the scene before him. Then he nodded. "Fairies. She's just so little—it has to be fairy magic."

"You know that they say, don't you? Never say thank you to the fae."

"And leave out little gifts like honey and milk for them."

"Never eat their food." I glanced pointedly at our plates, widening my eyes in mock horror. "Oh no."

Deacon shook with his held-in laughter, making a funny wheezing sound. Shye zeroed in on him almost immediately.

"Are you okay, Deacon?"

Deacon threw a hand up in a stop gesture. "I'm fine. Thank you."

He darted a look my way, eyebrows up and eyes wide in an exaggerated shocked face. I mimicked him, purposely trying to look slightly fearful.

Not laughing was really, really hard. "What did I tell you about saying thank you to the fae?"

He grimaced. "Looks like I'm indebted to her forever now."

I shook my head slowly, clucking my tongue. Still fighting hard not to laugh. "She owns your ass."

"Could be worse."

"How?"

"Alder could be the one owning my ass."

And with that, all attempts not to laugh failed. I absolutely howled, straight-up guffawed as the others in the room watched in amused befuddlement. Having no idea we'd just had an entire side conversation about magic and fairies and ridiculousness right there in their midst. Being with Deacon was just so much fun.

And that thought pulled me back to my senses. "Sorry," I said, waving off everyone else. "Deacon thinks he's a clown."

"A clown with an ass not owned by Alder Kennard. Can I get an amen?"

Elijah, Finn, Jinx, and I all raised our glasses and shouted amen. Shye didn't seem to catch on, but she grinned and looked to be enjoying the show. Alder frowned, obviously irritated at being the focus of our sarcasm. I considered that a win.

As the night wore on, people broke off into small groups and little pods to chat with one another. At one point, I noticed Finn and Deacon in what looked like a very serious discussion in the corner. I sat in an armchair, watching. Unable to look away. Elijah must have noticed because he sat his butt on the arm of my chair and leaned over me.

"What's got your attention, Lainie?"

I huffed. "I really hate that nickname."

"I know. Hence the usage of it."

I'd yell at him about that later. "What do you think that's all about?"

He followed my gaze to the sight of Deacon and Finn quite obviously arguing. Then he sighed. "Alder wants Finn and Jinx to leave town for the weekend."

"This weekend? Why?"

"Big brother thinks the bad guys are coming for us, so he wants to send a few select people off to...well, hide."

That sounded ominous. "We're supposed to stay here for the weekend."

Fuck Thanksgiving, Deacon had said. *Sunday morning—pack it up and head back to Denver where you'll be safe.*

Apparently, he wasn't the only one pushing for that.

Elijah sighed, sounding slightly defeated. "Yeah."

"So, what—we stick around and just wait to be slaughtered?"

"He wants you gone, too. So, no—I'll be the only one on the slaughtering end of things."

That did *not* make me feel better. "Again...why?"

"Again...bad guys."

"What can you do about bad guys that I can't? I'm a better shot than you."

He lifted a shoulder in surrender. "I'm not arguing that. And Finn's got excellent observation skills—he'd make a great lookout. Jinx too. But big bro says GTFO."

"So, Alder thinks he can just take out a whole slew of these guys alone."

"Not alone, but pretty much."

"He's an idiot."

"Some days."

Deacon and Finn finally broke apart, neither looking happy with whatever resolution they'd come to. Elijah jumped up to follow his twin, likely looking to make sure everything was smoothed over. I tracked Deacon as he headed into the kitchen.

"You wanted to do one more pass over the ridge area," he said, talking to Alder. Big brother had his wife on his lap and looked as if leaving was the last thing on his mind.

Alder flat-out sighed as if resigned to a fate he had no interest in. "Yeah, I did."

Ever observant, Deacon shrugged and laid on a hand on Alder's shoulder. "I can handle it. You stay here with Shye. You've been gone all day."

"Where are you going?" Elijah asked, approaching the trio.

Deacon looked his way. "Out to the ridge to put the drone in the air for surveillance."

"I'll go with you," Elijah said. That little flame of jealousy from earlier burned hotter and brighter, this time far more justified.

"I'm in too."

The entire room turned to look my way. Each and every person staring as if I'd just announced I was, indeed, fae.

I was as close to ready to cower as I'd ever been. "What?"

It was Finn who spoke up. "You're going too? Into the woods? At night?"

As if I was afraid. "Like I've never gone into the woods...*at night*. Come on. I grew up here just like the rest of you boys. I had you ignorant assholes as role models. I know how to piss behind a tree with the best of them. Let's go."

Deacon took control of the room with a simple statement. "That's all the skill I need to know about. Let's go, you two."

Finn suddenly looked to be biting back a smirk, but Alder...ooh, he looked mad. Not that I needed to care about that. I kept my head high and grabbed my jacket, slipping my boots on in the garage. They weren't exactly *hiking in the snow* sort of boots, but they'd do to keep my feet dry. Plus, there wasn't much snow around—the Front had gotten a good amount early in the season, but the warm spell they'd been having had melted most of it. I was more likely to run into mud puddles than snowbanks. I could deal with that.

Deacon led us out of the garage and into the dark, heading toward a big truck with four doors that immediately made me think the man was compensating for something smaller. Then I remembered...

Nope. He just liked big trucks.

"Shotgun," Elijah said, jogging around the front of the truck. "You're slow this week, Lainie girl."

I was going to kill that man.

"There's plenty of room in the back," Deacon said, lunging past me to open the rear driver's side door. "Let me get that for you."

"Thanks." I climbed inside, my entire body almost relaxing at the smell of the cab. I couldn't have pinpointed the scent of Deacon Manns on a shelf, but once I had it nearby? Once that scent hit me again? Pure memory overload. The man smelled good, and his scent lingered.

Elijah and Deacon climbed into the front seat, both chatting about the drone itself. Specs, how high it flew, GPS coordination, FAA regulations. This continued all the way up into the mountainside over Justice. Blacktop, dirt roads, concrete, rock paths —didn't matter. Deacon drove carefully and chatted casually, he and Elijah obviously comfortable with each other.

"This is where I was heading," Deacon said as he turned into a copse of trees, the pine branches rubbing against the side of the truck. The path ended in a small clearing, almost a meadow of sorts with little hills of snow still rimming it in what must have been an area that never saw direct sunlight. I would have played for hours in a place like this as a kid.

"It reminds me of the meadow up over the hill behind Daddy's house. Remember, Eli?"

"Yeah, I do." My brother turned a little in his seat. "Feeling homesick?"

For my parents? For the house we no longer lived in? For the carefree life I'd once had? "Absolutely."

Deacon put the truck in park, interrupting us. "Let's go, kids."

We piled out, and the men went to work, setting up the drone and tablet. I walked around the edge of the clearing, letting the night and the forest take me back. Remembering how soothing the silence of this area was. There was nothing like a winter in the mountains, the way everything just stopped and the entire world seemed to fall quiet. I hadn't thought about that in years, hadn't even considered coming home when I could end up snowed in.

Hadn't realized how much I missed the smell of cold on the Front until right at that moment.

"You ready, Lainie?" Elijah stood with the tablet in his hands, drone at his feet. He looked more excited than I'd seen him in months.

I could barely hold back my grin. "You find a new toy to play with?"

"Yes." Elijah hit a couple spots on the tablet, Deacon watching over his shoulder and whispering directions. The drone began to whir, lifting off the ground slowly. Rising straight up. Elijah piloted the thing with Deacon looking on. Me? I stood back and let the two figure this out. I had no interest in the drone itself, more in what it would find. If anything.

While the boys watched the screen, I settled in on the gate of the truck. I even lay back to watch the night sky, trying so hard to see the constellations I could never find. I knew they were there; I just didn't know enough about them to make out more than the Big Dipper.

"Stargazing?" Deacon sat down beside me, lying back and mimicking my position with about six inches between us. "See anything good?"

I raised my arm and pointed. "Big Dipper."

"Cool. What else?"

"That's all I know. Big Dipper."

He chuckled quietly, pointing. "If you keep looking north from the cup, there's another square with a triangular point on the one side and two little offshoots on the bottom. That—with the Big Dipper—makes up Ursa Major."

"The bear."

"Exactly. And Ursa Minor, or the Little Dipper, is right over—" he nudged my arm, aligning the line of sight to see another collection of stars that made a definite shape "—there."

"So, what's the third cup?"

"What third cup?"

It was my turn to grab his arm and realign it, moving so we were both pointing a little south and west from the smaller bear. "That cup."

"Ah. That's the constellation Draco."

I turned my head to look at him, my brow tightening. "Like from Harry Potter?"

"Yep. Like from Harry Potter. Draco the snake."

Fascinating. "Show me more."

So, he did, pointing out collections of stars I couldn't quite put together with names like Delphinus and Sagitta, Vulpecula and

Cygnus. All the while, he inched closer to me. Both of us laughing and looking and existing in the space together. Until his shoulder was right up against mine and our hands were no longer pointing but stacked atop one another, until my knee rested on his. Until we lay in silence, watching the night sky. There was a comfort in that moment that I hadn't had in a long while, a calmness and sense of security I hadn't even realized I had been missing.

But then Elijah started yelling.

"I found something!"

Deacon jackknifed up and was off the truck before I could even sit up, the man already running toward my brother by the time I had crawled off the tailgate. I followed at a slower pace, almost wishing Elijah hadn't seen anything. *Way to ruin the mood, brother.*

"I don't know this place," Deacon said, frowning at the screen. "That's definitely some sort of camp, though."

I took a spot on Elijah's opposite side, all three of us staring at the screen.

"Is that the ridge over there?" I pointed at a deeper shadow on the upper part of the screen.

"Yeah," Elijah said. "That's the ridge and that looks like the old logging road at the base, but I don't know this holler."

"I do." I shrugged when both men practically whipped their heads in my direction. "There's a rocky section just past the bowl that fills up with water in the summer during the snow melt in the mountains. Mercy and I used to go skinny-dipping there all the time."

Both men stared, not blinking. Elijah broke first with a loud laugh.

"That's actually fitting, really."

"What is?"

"That you and Mercy would go skinny-dipping together a lot. Did you forget you owned bathing suits?"

I shrugged. "Mom would have noticed if I came home every night with a wet suit, and then Daddy would have wanted to know exactly where we were and what we were up to. It was more fun to be sneaky."

Elijah elbowed Deacon. "See? Fitting."

But Deacon didn't smile or laugh. In fact, the man stood stock-still, staring at me hard.

"There're a lot of vehicles out there. I need to call Zane about this," Elijah said, stepping away and leaving me with Deacon as he rushed deeper into the meadow to talk about coordinates and targets and whatever else with Zane. I had no idea who *Zane* was or how Elijah knew him, but that didn't matter because I was obsessed with the look on Deacon's face.

"What's got you so quiet?" I whispered, inching closer to him.

"Thinking of you..."

The way his breathing increased, the raspy quality of his voice. I understood where his mind was in an instant.

"Thinking of me naked."

He exhaled hard as if breathing out all the desire I knew had to be burning through him. "Yeah."

Simple answer. Simple solution too.

I inched closer to him, keeping my voice low as I ran a finger up his hand. Subtle. So very subtle. "Too bad it's so cold. If it were summer, we could go skinny-dipping."

Deacon threw subtle out the window. He grabbed my arm and tugged me closer, angling us so his body hid mine from where Elijah paced a few yards away. He even dropped his head into my neck, breathing me in. Making me tremble in his hold.

"If we're making up perfect scenarios, then I'd rather take you some place warm. Some island in the Caribbean where we can fall asleep to the sounds of the waves."

"And you'd get me naked?"

His hold increased, his grip on me tightening. "Every fucking chance I could."

There was no rebuttal for that, no way to push back on his statement because I wanted that too. Wanted to experience days and weeks and months and years of being with the man. Of falling in love and enjoying the physicality that emotional connection brought with it. The two of us could disappear out into the world, alone with just each other.

If only. "Yeah, well—"

"Alder wants us to come back so he can look over the video," Elijah said, pulling up short when he noticed how close Deacon and I were standing. Deacon released my arm, his eyes still on mine but his body moving away. Leaving me behind. Again.

"Yeah. Okay. Recall the drone so we can get her packed up."

"Already on it." Elijah frowned my way then turned and walked toward the center of the meadow once more, leaving Deacon and me alone.

Apart and alone.

"Sorry," Deacon said, shaking his head. "I didn't mean to—"

"Yes, you did." I closed the space between us one last time, let my entire body rest against his. Grabbed his neck and dug my fingers into his flesh there so he felt me. "You did mean to, but Daddy's calling so you're pulling away again."

"Lainie, I—"

But I was done. I released him, walking toward the truck. Tired of the back-and-forth. "You keep dreaming of me naked, but don't be surprised when someone else gets to be the one in that island fantasy with me. I'm not waiting around for you."

I hopped onto the back of the truck again, lying back to stare at the stars for a bit longer. This time, when someone settled in next to me, it was my brother.

"You good?" Elijah asked, his voice quiet but concerned.

"Yeah…just distracted."

He grunted as if in approval but stayed silent for a few minutes as the hum of the drone moved closer, as the night sky sat twinkling above us. As he apparently thought a few things over.

"Hey, sis?"

I turned to look his way. "Yeah?"

"Stop letting Alder get in your way. He's your biggest obstacle for some reason, and it's time to either go around him, go over him, and go the fuck through him."

"If only it were that easy." I sighed, the rightness of what he was saying sitting heavy on my chest. "Who's Zane?"

"Friend of Alder and Deacon's."

"A friend you call about drone footage."

"Yeah."

I nodded, puzzle pieces beginning to land. "Hey, Eli?"

"Yeah?"

"Maybe you should take your own advice."

Elijah dropped his hand on my leg, giving me a squeeze before rising to sitting once more. "Not the same situation, sister dear, but message heard."

"You two ready?" Deacon slipped in beside the truck, setting the drone into a big plastic box that he then secured to the side of the bed.

Go around, go over, or go through. Right. Good advice...for someone else.

"Sure," I said. "Let's hit the road."

Chapter Nine

DEACON

No one likes waking up and immediately needing to jack off. No adult, anyway. But that was the situation when I woke up Monday morning after spending the evening in the heaven and hell that the Kennard family had become for me. So, I rolled my ass out of bed, headed for the bathroom, and spent the next fifteen minutes soaping myself down. Me and Rosy Palm, together again.

Just the two of us...

I got ready for my day while my mind spun, though not with plans for the Soul Suckers. Instead, I could not stop thinking about the night before. All that time spent with Lainie. The second she'd mentioned having been skinny-dipping in the pond by the camp we'd found, I'd been besieged by visions of that luscious body sans clothing. Not an imaginary version either. No, sir. I'd experienced that woman, so I knew exactly what every inch looked like. I got locked in my own mind, replaying the night we'd been together and changing the background, the location, the positions to suit whatever I wanted. Beach scene? Done. Mountain chalet with a fireplace warming her naked skin? Easy. Naked Lainie in an apartment with a view of the Eiffel Tower. Not even close to a challenge.

We'd gone back to Alder's after our little recon mission, and even being around my best friend hadn't calmed my imagination. While I should have been focusing on Alder and his plotting and planning for the Soul Suckers camp, I stayed lost in nearly pornographic images of his sister and me doing horribly sexy things. Memories, dreams, debauched thoughts of the stuff I would do to Lainie Kennard if she were truly mine.

The man would have killed me on sight if he'd gotten even a glimpse of what had played through my head while I'd been in his house. Hell, all four of her brothers likely would have. She was their baby sister, and I was a man who didn't deserve to put his dirty hands on her.

Lainie Kennard. Not mine, not a baby, and not likely to give a flying fuck that she was slowly destroying my life.

"Sounds about right."

Once I had decent control of the blood pumping to my dick and relatively clean thoughts in my head, I hopped in my truck and drove across town to Alder's place. We were meeting—yes, again. This time, with the entire team to discuss what would be coming next, which meant spending a lot of time in his barn. With the Kennard brothers. The ones who would likely kill me if...

"That thought's been on repeat all morning," I said to myself as I shut off the ignition. "Get your shit together, Manns."

I hiked my way over to the barn, waving to Shye when she came to the window. It wasn't that I didn't want to run in and joke with her a bit—pick on that husband of hers a few times—but I couldn't run the risk of running into Lainie and losing what little control I had over my brain. So directly to the barn I went.

"About time you made it," Bishop said as soon as I walked inside the old building. "He's being a grumpy asshole."

"When isn't he?"

Bishop laughed and led the way to where Alder stood, where he and I had once killed two men for daring to threaten his Shye. Seemed fitting we'd return to the scene of that crime to plot another one.

"I don't want you distracted," Alder said, sounding frustrated. As if he'd repeated those words a number of times already. Knowing him, he likely had.

"Jinx and I aren't going anywhere," Finn said. The man looked solid and sure. Not at all threatened or intimidated by the energy of his big brother. Which was good—Alder could be an imposing figure. Lots of people made the decision to back down from him based solely on that aura of power. Finn wasn't.

I knew I liked that kid.

"What's happening here?" I slipped in beside Alder, looking from Finn to him and back again.

Alder huffed. "Finn doesn't want to leave town."

"I can fight just like the rest of you."

I shrugged. "He can."

Alder didn't look thrilled that I was backing his little brother. "I know he can, but he also needs to be protected."

Elijah stepped in next to his twin, the two facing off against Alder in what looked like a united front. "No more so than anyone else here. If Finn wants to stay, he should stay. None of us would be able to live with ourselves if anything happened to someone we cared about and we weren't here to at least try to help."

Alder sighed, turning to pace the length of the room. "Some of you are likely to be more distracted than others. That's the only reason—"

"I'm staying too," Bishop said, coming to stand beside his twin brothers. Three against one. "My family and friends are safest if I'm here to watch over them. We're not leaving town."

Alder froze in place, appearing stunned. "You'll be distracted."

"SEALs don't get distracted. Besides, if I start worrying about anything other than the mission at hand, Gage will kick some sense into me."

"True facts," the big mechanic said, nodding toward his best friend. "I've got his back."

I didn't wait for Alder to reply. "Well, now that that's all settled, who wants to watch some drone footage from last night?"

The guys slowly agreed, peeling off to find a comfortable spot around the screen Alder had apparently set up.

"You just happened to have all this equipment lying around?" I asked as I started the process of setting up my tablet to play through his projector. I figured discussing projectors and screens would be a good distraction from the fact that he'd just lost a fight with his brothers.

Alder seemed nonplussed. "Shye and I like to watch a lot of movies."

I wasn't about to ask what kind, but a flash of possibility leaped into my head. Lainie and me and a camera...film just for us.

Alder coughed, and all thoughts other than "plug cord into machine" flew away, to be reviewed later.

Once the tech setup was complete, I settled into a folding chair and began truly analyzing the film. In that little campground area, there were eight vehicles, three larger than a standard SUV. Assuming those larger ones seated eight and the others seated five at most, we were looking at—

"Fifty men," Gage said, obviously following my thoughts. "Looks like at most about fifty men."

"Yeah." I exhaled long and loud. If we were right, we were really outnumbered. Even with half that amount, the likelihood of running into manpower issues was high. "We can't do this alone."

"Who are you thinking about?" Alder asked, looking just as concerned as the rest of us.

There was really only one answer. "Zane's group."

"You think he'd be willing?"

Elijah responded before I had the chance to. "He'd be willing."

I raised an eyebrow at the kid but didn't comment. Zane had been my contact, but apparently Elijah had taken over owning that relationship. That was fine so long as his crew was available to help us. Zane was a good guy—honest and loyal and in law enforcement, which meant we got lots of heads-ups when we needed them. He had a team of people that worked with him, all of whom had various— and impressive—skills. His demolition expert alone could clear a path for us if needed.

We spent the next thirty minutes reviewing the footage and reaching out to Zane to set up another planning session with them. We made sure his team knew where the threat was hunkered down so there was no accidental crossing of paths. We also decided Elijah would head back out with my drone to grab some daytime shots if possible. That would be harder because, while the flying contraption was awfully stealthy, it still made a whirring noise that could possibly be heard from the ground.

"Ambient noise of the forest in the daytime should cover me," Elijah said, looking far more excited than he should have been. "I'll be careful."

"You just want to play with the toy."

The man's grin was wider and brighter than I'd ever seen from him. "It's just so cool."

Yeah, it sort of was.

Once we had our marching orders and a solid rotation of watchers for Main Street and all of our vulnerable population, once the phone tree had been started to make sure everyone in Justice knew to be extra careful, we headed back toward the house. Shye met us on the porch, but she wasn't alone.

"You guys done being Masters of the Universe back there?" Lainie shot us all a sarcastic sort of smile, one that didn't hold an ounce of happiness. She didn't like being left out of things. Not at all.

"You been behaving yourself?" Alder asked, making her smile drop and her irritation show through even brighter.

"I'm not a child."

"Never said you were."

There was a huff and an eye roll, though Alder was already back in Shye's orbit, so I doubted if he noticed either. I saw, though. I noticed.

Sadly, there was nothing I could do about it.

"Zane wants to meet up," Elijah said, looking down at his phone and totally interrupting the moment. "You in, Deacon?"

I nodded, still watching Lainie, who suddenly seemed really interested in what we were talking about. "I'll drive."

"Cool. Lainie, I—"

"I know, I know. You have stuff to do." She rose to her feet, stretching in a way that made all the blood in my body flow south before striding our way. "So, where are you going anyway?"

Elijah had walked away while the other guys stood on the porch with Alder and Shye. That left just her and me standing by my truck. Alone and yet not.

Fuck, I could almost sense I was about to lose...something. "Elijah and I need to go see a man about a thing."

"A thing," she said, putting emphasis on both syllables in a way that screamed her doubt.

"Yeah, a thing."

"What sort of thing?"

"The sort of thing you shouldn't know about."

The woman was an evil temptress, stepping closer and lowering her voice. Looking up at me through her long lashes with an expression that was both sensual and innocent all at once.

"But I like to know things, Deacon."

Sorceress. "I'm aware of this fact."

I swallowed hard, trying not to let my body betray me. Fighting the urge to grab her by her hips and pick her up so I could press my body to hers. So I could pin her against the side of the truck and show her how much I knew about what she liked.

"So, Deacon," she said, inching closer. "Is this thing dangerous?"

"Not really, no."

The evil queen of my kingdom shrugged one shoulder, looking nearly disinterested as she said, "Then take me with you."

Those manipulation skills were downright impressive. "What did you say?"

"I said..." She smiled, giving away how much fun she was having at my expense. "Take me with you. If it's not dangerous, there's no reason I can't tag along."

Elijah slipped in beside us. "She's got a point. And I call shotgun."

Alder was going to kill me, and then Bishop would have his turn. There would be no surviving the Kennard boys once they figured out how weak I was when it came to their sister.

Fuck me, but if I was going down, I might as well do it in style.

"Fine by me." I took a step back, putting much-needed space between Lainie and me before looking to Alder and raising my voice. "I've got the youngest two with me."

My best friend looked downright confused. "You're taking both Lainie and Elijah to meet Zane?"

"Yup." I headed for the driver's side door, once again opening the back one for Lainie like the gentleman I knew I definitely wasn't. "Hop in, kids. It's a motherfucking party up in here."

Chapter Ten

LAINIE

Being in the truck with Elijah and Deacon was becoming my happy place. An odd thought, to be sure, but I was far more comfortable around the two men than anywhere else in Justice. Plus, they liked to chat quietly and joke around. It was fun to see Elijah—my usually straitlaced and all business brother—so relaxed. Being in Justice was good for him.

Deacon pulled off the highway and onto a dirt road, following it to another clearing. This one was smaller, barely enough room to turn the vehicle around if he wanted to, but it wasn't empty. Another truck was already there, facing us. Sitting still and silent in the shadows of the trees.

"Is that them?" I asked, my hands trembling a bit as I tried really hard to tamp down my nerves.

"Yup." Deacon unbuckled himself then grabbed a handgun out of the console. "We're safe with them, but I don't take chances."

Good to know.

The three of us exited the truck and walked toward the other vehicle. Three people matching us—two men, one woman—met us in the clearing. The moment was quiet, surreal almost. Anticipation weighed on me like a blanket, and I practically had to clamp my knees together to keep my legs from shaking. I was a mess, though I really didn't think I was showing it.

Deacon was flat-out calm. "Brought some of your team, I see."

The man at the front of the other group, with the thick black glasses and jeans so dark and stiff they looked as if he'd starched them, peered our way. His eyes landed on me, his face staying glacial and firm. No sign of emotion. No interest or disinterest. Just...nothing. So disconcerting.

"You didn't come alone either."

Deacon shrugged. "They're Kennards. I trust them."

Those dark eyes landed on me again, this time taking a slow perusal from top to bottom. Heat rushed up my neck, that tendency to blush from when I was a child suddenly reappearing as this man— this stranger—definitely took in an eyeful. But I wasn't a child anymore, and I was certainly used to being ogled. Maybe not by a man likely carrying a gun, but still. This was not new.

I cocked an eyebrow when his eyes once again met mine. "Get a good enough look, friend?"

A slow smile spread across the man's face, ending just as a chuckle broke out. "She's a Kennard, all right. Got more BDE than all her brothers put together, I'd guess."

Deacon glanced my way, positively smirking. "You would be correct on that one, Zane."

I had no idea what BDE meant, and being left out of the joke definitely didn't do anything to stop my temper from flaring. I kept my mouth shut, though, because whatever had just happened seemed to have broken the ice. Deacon and glasses guy—Zane, apparently— met at the halfway point, shaking hands. Even Elijah joined in. I stayed back, watching. Wary and uncomfortable...and slightly obsessed with Deacon's change in demeanor.

Gone was the casual bartender or friendly guy cracking jokes and flirting. In his place was a new man. One who had definitely done stuff like this before. One with a strong voice, a command of the situation, and no fear of talking about weapons and casualties and highway checkpoints. Deacon the military man was before me, and I liked what I saw. A lot.

I wonder what he'd look like in a uniform.

Knowing this was neither the time nor the place to get distracted by Deacon being all manly and intense, I turned away from the meeting happening and took in the nature around me. Trees that were likely centuries-old towered above me, making the sunlight land on the ground in dapples instead of beams. I stared off past the other truck, taking in the hillside behind them. The road must have eventually ended in a ridge or something, because there was clearly another hill behind them. Either that or we were on the top of a hill, and continuing forward would have brought us to another slope. Whatever—the view was amazing and filled with sunlight and trees and a single light flashing now and again.

A single light flashing...

As Deacon, Zane, and Elijah continued chatting about something to do with scopes and suppressors, I took a few steps forward. Really looking hard at that hill opposite us. The woman with Zane—a redhead with thick lips and big, round sunglasses covering her eyes—turned with me. Watching me, it appeared. Not that I gave a shit. Not really.

"Do you see that?" I asked once I stood almost next to her.

The woman blinked then stepped closer, following my gaze. "See what?"

"That flash of light."

She stood silent for a moment, both of us staring. When the thing flashed again, I glanced her way.

The woman did not appear to be concerned. "Maybe it's a bird or something."

I shook my head, frowning and squinting toward the other hillside once more. "Birds don't reflect light."

Unable to stop myself, I walked farther into the woods, needing to get a better view of that hill. Wishing I had a pair of binoculars so I could see what the heck was reflecting the sunlight. While it could have been nothing—a window from a hunting cabin or a wet rock placed just right—my gut told me there was something more over there. Something that could be dangerous. Something I should be worried about.

Without warning, Deacon appeared at my side. I smelled his cologne a moment before his shoulder brushed mine.

"What's wrong?"

I nearly shivered at the tone in his voice, the deep, gritty sound of concern washing over me.

"How do you know something's wrong?"

"I can read it in your body."

As if. "You think you can read my body now?"

He looked down at me, those dark eyes dropping past mine to get a good look at...well, my body. "I know I can, so what's up?"

I turned my attention back to the hill, pointing with one arm. "Watch there."

We stood in silence, both of us staring across the ravine. In a matter of seconds, the light flashed again. In a different place.

"What the..." Deacon took a step forward, his brow furrowed deeply.

I was frozen in place, knowing full well that whatever was reflecting the sunlight was not stationary.

"It's moving." I grabbed Deacon's arm, tucking myself underneath it so I could hold my point to the spot where the light had just flashed. "Wait for it."

We waited again, this time tucked together in a way that was far more sexual than I'd intended. His body felt warm against mine, every breath pressing him in tighter. Fast, deep breaths. He'd claimed he could read my body. Well, I could read his too. The man was aroused, likely also a little unnerved. He had a tension in his stance, an energy much like what I had to imagine a predator about to stalk his prey felt. Hard and stiff and ready to pounce at the slightest—

The light flashed again, a solid ten yards from where it had been before.

"Fuck." Deacon grabbed my hand and spun us, running toward the clearing and the men who were obviously interested in what we were doing. "Someone's watching us."

Zane was in motion before Deacon finished speaking, running to the door of his truck. "Details, beret."

"Light flare in motion on the opposite hill. Could be binoculars or a scope. My guess is a scope." Deacon grabbed another gun from his truck, a long, scary-looking rifle this time. "Tuck in behind the vehicles. Zane, I expect you to get everyone out if things go sideways."

Zane nodded once, standing just at the bumper of his own truck. "Understood."

Deacon pushed me along, making sure I was planted firmly on the opposite side of his truck before turning back to Zane. Not that I was ready to let Deacon just run off, though.

"What are you going to do?" I asked, clinging to his hand.

Deacon looked down at where I'd grabbed him then back up at my face, a distracted sort of conflict in his expression. "I'm going to do what I do best."

With that, he was gone, running off into the woods. Disappearing into the brush.

"What is he going to do?" I asked, leaning against Elijah as we all stared in the direction he'd headed.

It was Zane who answered me. "He's going to do what he does best."

I was really irritated to hear that same answer again. "But what's that?"

Zane pointed, making me look higher into the treetops. Forcing my gaze up. "He was a sniper in the military—he's heading for higher ground to get a solid view of what's happening."

Higher ground...or higher vantage point. No ropes, just Deacon and a tree that could sway with any breeze, that could be dried or dead or damaged. One that could have a widow-maker trapped high up in the branches. The man hadn't been brought up around the lumber industry—he might not know how dangerous the forest could be. How one branch trapped in the canopy and just the right breeze could steal his life before he could get out of its path. Could drop him in an instant.

I was going to be sick. "All alone?"

No one answered me, but they also didn't move. Not my brother, not this Zane guy, or the man he'd brought with him. Not the redhead. No one. I couldn't let Deacon take all the risk alone.

Without a word, I raced after him, ignoring Elijah's calls for me to stop and wait. No way would I do either, not when Deacon could need someone to watch out for him. Even if he just fell and sprained an ankle, the man could need assistance. I wasn't some newbie hiker in the woods—I knew better than to go off alone without some form of backup notification to let people know if I was in trouble. The woods around Justice were gorgeous and kept most of the town employed and fed. They'd also kill you in an instant.

I wasn't letting Deacon die alone on a hillside.

Tracking Deacon wasn't as hard as it could have been. The man left a solid trail through the underbrush that any good hunter could have followed. I was apparently a good hunter because I came upon him after just a few minutes of searching, locking eyes on the dark pants he'd been wearing before the rest of him because he was…lying down. But above my eye level.

"Did you climb a tree?"

Deacon shot me a very irritated look. "What are you doing here?"

I leaned against a tree to the side of the one he'd planted himself in, crossing my arms and doing my best to appear far more casual than I felt as I scanned the canopy above him.

"I didn't like the idea of you dying alone in the woods, so I followed you."

He coughed a rough laugh. "You interested in dying with me?"

"If that's what I need to do, then yes."

Those green eyes pinned me in place, the look on his face one I'd never seen before. Intense, dark, and predatory. Deacon was on the hunt.

"You've got that Kennard bravery, that's for sure." He turned to refocus on the world in front of him, leaning down to peer through the scope on the rifle in his grip. We were silent for a few moments, both of us looking out over the ravine. Neither doing anything more than breathing.

At least until a memory distracted me from the moment. "You and Zane said I had the Kennard BDE earlier."

"You've got that, too."

I bit my lip, hating to admit when I didn't know something but absolutely desperate to get the joke. "What's BDE?"

Deacon didn't look away from his scope as he said, "Big dick energy."

I took a good couple of seconds to let that sink in. Growing up with all brothers, I understood the absolute obsession with that particular part of their anatomy, but I still hadn't ever thought about it in terms of my own personality or traits. I mean, I didn't have a dick, so having BDE was not something I would have thought of. Ever.

I couldn't argue with the concept, though. "Apparently I get the Kennard everything. Minus the respect."

Deacon grunted, keeping his eyes locked on his scope. "They want to protect you. It's instinctual."

"Because I'm the youngest?"

"Because you're a woman. There's a reason enemies use women as suicide bombers and spies." He leaned into his gun more, obviously focused on what he saw there. "Our culture teaches us you're the weaker sex, and unlearning that lesson takes time and energy most men simply don't care to exert."

"You think we're the weaker sex?"

"Hell no. I've watched women go through hours of unthinkable pain to give birth then start cleaning up after themselves within half an hour. I've had a female teammate pick me up and fireman-carry me out of a jungle. I've watched a woman who was brutalized by the men in her village rise up and kill ten of her aggressors without blinking an eye. And I've watched you stand firm against your brothers in ways that defy logic and for reasons I empathize with. You're not weak, beautiful. Deadly as fuck, but not weak."

There wasn't anything to say back to that. Not really. Not when he had a job to do up in that tree and I couldn't help him. But the second he was back on solid earth, the moment I knew we were safe, I was going to thank him for seeing me. Maybe with words, maybe with a kiss. I'd need to figure out the details once my head stopped spinning.

He truly saw me.

"It's a Soul Sucker," Deacon said, reclaiming my attention. "He's got a patch on the back of his jacket. Looks like binoculars in his hand, not a gun."

"Are you sure?"

"Roger that." He sat silent for a few more minutes, his body tense but so very still. "He's looking all over, not directly at us. Can you text Elijah and let him know? Tell him they can stay calm—it doesn't look like they've spotted us."

I grabbed my phone out of my pocket, typing away as I asked, "Are they in danger?"

"I don't think so."

"How can you tell?"

"Gut instinct."

That was...not reassuring. "What if your gut is wrong?"

He didn't reply. Not for a solid minute. He just stayed silent, staring through the scope. Tense and waiting for...something.

I had no patience. "Deacon. What if your gut is wrong?"

No answer again.

I rephrased the question, lowering my voice a little. Trying hard to stay calm. "Has your gut ever been wrong?"

His jaw ticked, his attention obviously captured. "Yeah. Once."

"What happened?"

"People died, and your brother was shot," he said, so quiet I almost didn't hear him. Almost.

"So, what if it's wrong now?" Because Elijah was back at that truck with only Zane and his two teammates to keep him safe. And while I trusted Deacon's judgment, those people weren't Kennards. They weren't from Justice.

They weren't kin.

"Deacon, I—"

"Let's go back." He rose to his knees on the branch, grabbing his gun with one hand and supporting himself on the drop down with the other. "We need to get to the truck."

"That's it?" I glanced around, totally confused by the switch from sniper to runner. "No firing a warning shot or...a not-so-warning shot?"

Deacon grabbed my hand, tugging me after him. "The guy is looking around but not at us. He may be a guard, or he may be a man out in the woods watching birds. I'm not killing a man for taking a walk in the mountains without knowing how many others are standing behind him."

"But you said he's a Soul Sucker."

"Yeah, I did. And they usually don't travel alone. I'm not kicking off a war without knowing the full situation."

I was lost in his thought process, but I didn't fight back. Instead, I followed behind him, clinging to his hand and trying hard not to slow him down. We reached the clearing in almost no time, finding the rest of the group once again standing between the two trucks, all eyes focused on us.

"So?" Zane said, a definite question in his voice.

"One guy," Deacon said, still not letting go of my hand. "Definitely a Soul Sucker but the flash was binoculars, not a scope. And he wasn't focused anywhere in particular. He was scanning the woods."

"Think he's a scout?"

"More than likely a guard, but I couldn't tell for sure."

Zane frowned but nodded. "Good call on retreating, then. There's no telling how many others are on the back side of that ridge."

Deacon grunted. "I say we get out of here. Let's head to the bar to finish up our conversation and work out the plans. We saw their setup at night—we can use that footage."

"Fine," Zane said, already heading for his truck. "But I have bible study tonight, so this can't be an all-night thing."

I couldn't let that go. "You go to bible study?"

Zane stopped hard, turning slowly to face me. "Why wouldn't I?"

I shrugged, totally thrown off by this aspect of the man with the gun and the plan. "It doesn't fit what I thought I knew of you, is all."

Zane took a step closer, truly stabbing me with his stare. "And the great dragon was thrown down, that ancient serpent, who is called the devil and Satan, the deceiver of the whole world—he was thrown down to the earth, and his angels were thrown down with him."

I swallowed hard, needing to cough slightly before responding. "Therefore rejoice, O heavens and you who dwell in them! But woe to you, O earth and sea, for the devil has come down to you in great wrath, because he knows that his time is short!"

Zane continued to stare my way, silent and still along with all the others. Even Deacon said nothing, just kept his place beside me with my hand in his.

Finally, Zane nodded. "I was right about you."

"How so?"

He grinned, looking so much like some long-passed fifties rock star, it took my breath away. "Big dick energy. You practically glow with it like your brother over there." He gave Elijah a nod. "Meet you at the bar."

And with that, Zane and his team hurried to their truck. Deacon led me to his, opening the back door for me and leaning in once I was settled.

"You continue to amaze me at every turn."

I lifted a shoulder, trying hard to look casual. "I'm full of surprises."

He laughed, reaching out to pat my thigh. "No shit, beautiful. I picked up on that real quick."

He shut my door then hopped into the driver's seat, not even bothering to turn the truck around but instead throwing it into reverse. Elijah looked over his shoulder at me, eyebrows raised. I sat back, tossing a wink his way. His lips turned up into a smirk that spoke volumes.

He knew.

He knew Deacon and I had a *thing*.

He might not have figured out how far that thing had gone, but he knew something was there.

Whether he decided to be a tattletale or a wingman was still up in the air.

Chapter Eleven

DEACON

Lainie Kennard was going to be the death of me.

I'd known that since the night I'd met her. Since the morning when I had figured out Elaine was Lainie and I'd just slept with my best friend's little sister. I'd been convinced of it when she'd come back to town looking like a meal I wanted to devour and tossing me those sexy smirks. She was a strong, beautiful woman who would likely kick my ass to the curb before giving me a chance to apologize for making mistakes, destroying my life in the process.

And I was falling more in love with her by the second.

"Let's go," I said once I had the truck in park outside the Jury Room. I didn't want anyone exposed for long, not with Soul Suckers in the woods. So, I made sure Elijah and Lainie followed me inside, shutting the door behind us once we were within the familiar walls of the bar I'd bought, grown, and loved for all my time in Justice. The one that had technically been closed for months at that point. "Anyone want a drink?"

"I'll take a beer," Elijah said before hooking his thumb at Lainie. "She'll have whatever vodka drink you can make."

"Martini or like vodka and cranberry?"

My beautiful obsession shrugged one shoulder, looking highly uninterested. "Surprise me."

"Surprise her," Elijah said, rolling his eyes. "Meanwhile, Lainie dear, we need to talk real quick."

The two disappeared down the back hallway, leaving me alone in the bar and having absolutely no idea what the fuck was going on.

"'Surprise me,' she says." I shook my head and rounded the bar, grabbing bottles along the way. "I'll surprise the fuck out of you, beautiful."

I headed to what I considered my office and grabbed a few bottles. A quick run into the back kitchen to grab some sort of milk product—individual coffee creamer tubs, best I could do—and I was mixing. Crème de cacao, chocolate liqueur, a good splash of vanilla vodka, all poured into the shaker along with a bunch of ice. The coffee creamer, I added last, hoping like hell it didn't curdle or separate. I cursed myself for not having actual half and half on hand, but what could I say? The bar had been closed for months. Dairy products had not been my priority.

I did have chocolate syrup, though. I poured some on a plate and rolled the rim of the glass through it, being careful to make sure it dripped only on the inside. Once the glass was ready, I shook that shaker as hard as I could. Lainie and Elijah reappeared from the back in the middle of my shake, both looking at me with curious eyes, Elijah almost seemed to be holding back a smile. Something in his expression, in the way his eyes held mine, told me all I needed about what had just happened. He knew. I didn't know how or if things were about to go sideways, but the fucker knew about Lainie and me.

Death by Kennards...it was a true fear.

"What are you making there, barkeep?" Elijah asked as he settled onto a stool in front of me. I set down the shaker and handed him a beer, using a key to pop the cap off the bottle. Keeping my eyes on him in case he decided to pull a gun on me.

"I'm surprising your sister. Sorry it's bottled—I haven't ordered kegs since we've been closed."

The youngest Kennard son shrugged, not hesitating to grab the bottle. Not looking as if he were ready to jump across the bar and beat my ass either. "I'll take what I can get."

The door opened at that moment, and Zane walked through. His eyes immediately found Elijah, and he stutter-stepped. Just once, a tiny sort of stumble, but I saw it. I also saw the way Lainie took the seat beside her brother, how she flipped her hair over her shoulder and ran a finger along the corner of her mouth. Forget anything the men had to say, I had my entertainment and priority for the evening. I'd watch that woman simply exist and be fucking thrilled about it.

More nervous than I'd ever been in such a situation, I poured her drink and slipped it across the bar. Zane and Elijah were greeting each other, but I stayed focused on Lainie in that moment. I only had a few seconds to make my point.

"Your drink," I said, keeping my voice low.

Lainie took one look at the glass, and that same corner of her mouth she'd just had her finger against curled up all sexy and slow. She glanced at me, beautiful blue eyes stabbing into mine.

"You remembered."

As if I could forget.

"Deacon," Zane said, stealing my attention from the woman before me. "We need to get a visual on that hillside. See if there's another camp set up there."

I nodded, my focus splitting and shifting. Trying hard to pay attention to him. "Yeah. Of course. We can use my drone for that."

"Perfect." Zane turned once again toward Elijah, the two talking numbers and times and daylight. I gave no fucks. Zero. Lainie Kennard was in my bar, looking like a goddess among swine and drinking the martini I'd made her.

"Does it meet your expectations?" I asked, keeping my voice low and soft. Only for her.

She gave me that pirate smile again. "It's delicious."

"High praise from a woman such as yourself."

"I think we have enough time to get what we need now," Elijah said, once again stealing my focus. "Deacon and I can go if it'll be cutting too close to bible study."

I looked up at the mention of my name, knowing I needed to pay those two more attention but not wanting to. Thankfully, Zane shook his head.

"I've got a good two hours before I really need to head out."

"Great." Elijah hopped to his feet, finally looking my way. Appearing almost confused. *I know how you feel, kid.* "Uh, Zane and I can handle this. Unless you want to come to keep an eye on the drone."

Drone, schmone. "Nah, it's fine. You can take the toy out for a playdate."

Zane chuckled. "He gets really excited about that flying robot."

"It's fascinating technology," Elijah said, laughing in a good-natured sort of way. As if the teasing had been expected and almost welcomed. "Come on. Let's get out there."

He jerked to a stop when he left his seat, eventually spinning to peer at his sister. "Do you want to come, Lainie?"

I grabbed a towel and wiped down a glass, already reaching for a bottle behind me. I knew what she was going to say. Had no doubts she'd turn them down.

Lainie didn't disappoint. "Oh no. I've had enough time in the woods today."

Elijah glanced at me. "You can stay with her? Or should I—"

"I've got her," I said, fighting back the need to puff up my chest at that thought. "I'll stay with her here or take her home if she wants. You worry about the footage."

"You okay with that, sis?"

Lainie took another sip of her martini, running her tongue across her top lip in an oddly nonsexual and yet totally exaggerated sort of way. "I have martinis and Deacon for company. I'm all set."

Elijah shook his head and chuckled. "Good luck, man."

I took that to be directed at me. "You too. Let me know if you need anything."

He and Zane left together, the two diving into talk of calculations and best locations to launch from. I forgot all about them the second the door swung closed.

"No way I could forget," I said, dropping a few ice cubes into the glass before me.

Lainie raised an eyebrow—just one, I loved that trick—and pulled her martini glass away from her lips. "Forget what?"

"You sounded shocked that I remembered the chocolate martinis. There's no forgetting that night."

She reached for her glass, nodding toward the liquor bottles behind me. "This trip down memory lane only works if you're drinking an old-fashioned."

She wasn't wrong. That's what I'd been drinking the night we met—a bourbon old-fashioned. She'd sat down next to me and ordered a chocolate martini. The rest, as they say, was history.

History that shouldn't be repeated.

And yet, I poured a couple ounces of bourbon into my glass. "I don't have any simple syrup sitting around, but I think I have some crappy mix that will mimic it."

"So, I get a phenomenal drink—and it really is excellent—and you get a crappy one. Seems fair."

I let out a quick laugh and shook my head, reaching for the same crappy mix I'd mentioned. "It certainly does, princess."

"From beautiful to princess. You'll do anything to avoid calling me by my name tonight."

I rolled my eyes, making sure to give her a solid grin to keep from pissing her off. "I'll call you whatever you want me to, but in my head, you'll always be a beautiful princess."

"Which makes you what? The handsome prince?"

I took my drink—sans simple syrup and orange rind—and walked around the bar, coming to sit next to her. On her left, just like that night.

"I'll never be a prince, Lainie. I'm just the guard at the king's gate, trying my hardest to keep everyone in the castle safe."

"Including the princess."

"*Especially* the princess." I took a sip of my drink, the sting of the bourbon a quick reminder. The taste of cherries something I'd forever associate with the woman beside me. "God, I haven't had one of these since that night. I've missed it."

"You haven't been drinking?"

"Oh, no. I've been drinking. Rye whiskey, mostly."

"Why not your old-fashioned if you like it so much?"

I took another sip and licked my top lip, breathing in that cherry essence. "Reminds me too much of you."

She froze, watching me. Her expression falling. We sat in silence for a long moment, both of us studying the other, neither saying a word. I assumed she was remembering the same things I was—the drinks, the flirting, the drive to her hotel, the anticipation. The fantastic sex. Yeah, that night was etched into my mind—I didn't need a beverage to remind me of it. Especially when a repeat was damned near impossible.

A very sobering thought.

I turned my gaze to my drink, staring into the amber liquid while I asked, "How's school going, Lainie?"

She laughed, practically spilling her drink. "Talk about an awkward transition."

"Sorry. I just...wanted to have a regular conversation with you."

Her eyes locked on mine when I looked up, her gaze softening a bit. And then she sighed.

"Regular conversation. I can do that. I'm pretty much done with my MA. There's one last grade I'm waiting for, but unless I flat-out failed the presentation, I'm finished with classes and graduating in the spring."

I nodded, sort of knowing what her degrees were in, but barely. And only because I'd looked that shit up after I had actually met the woman. "So, you're going to become a social media influencer."

"No. I'm going to be the person responsible for finding, evaluating, and hiring the influencers, then taking advantage of any viral content to help scale the business that hires me."

I had gone to school—had even earned a bunch of letters after my name. I still felt far outpaced by the woman sitting next to me. "You're so fucking smart."

Lainie sighed, frowning into her glass. "Not according to my brothers. At least, not Alder or Bishop. They see what I do as playing online."

"Nah. Okay, maybe Alder. But Bishop does enough marketing to know better." I set down my drink, turning a bit to look at her head on. "Or at least, he should. If they don't understand the power of social media marketing at this point, they're idiots."

She reached out, setting her hand on mine. Making my entire body feel as if it were about to go up in flames.

"That's the sweetest thing anyone has ever said to me."

I laughed. Not subtle, not quiet, and definitely not a chuckle. I howled. This woman was something else.

"You're likely to be the death of me, Elaine Kennard."

The world went still, Lainie's face taking on a shocked expression. Fuck, I'd slipped and good. I couldn't call her that, couldn't think of her as that. Lainie or beautiful or princess—nothing else. And definitely never *that*.

I hopped to my feet and rushed toward the door, needing a distraction. "I should have locked this when Zane and Elijah left. I'm getting sloppy with my security in my old age."

"You're not old, Deacon."

But I was—too old for her, too old to throw my life into disarray the way I'd need to if I wanted her in it, too old to start over. Or at least, that's what I kept telling myself.

As I turned the latch on the door, locking us inside, music began to play. I spun, finding Lainie still sitting at the bar, her phone in her hand and a song coming from it. Some old thing I'd likely heard a thousand times with a jazzy sort of melody and a fresh piano riff leading the way. A new take on an old standard.

"Old can be better than new, you know." Lainie slipped off her seat, setting her phone on the bar and moving toward me. Closing the distance between us with slow, measured steps. "You didn't dance with me at the wedding."

Restraint, broken. Loyalty, shifted. Lainie Kennard was the only Kennard who mattered in that moment, the only person I needed and cared about. Fuck whatever the future would hold; I wanted to live in the look that beautiful princess was sending me.

I also wanted to erase all the shit I'd put her through and make it up to her.

I shook my head, my body moving toward hers of its own volition. "I couldn't."

"Wouldn't, not couldn't. We could have danced without giving ourselves away."

I reached for her, grabbing her hips and tugging her against me, unable to resist feeling her body pressed against mine for a second more.

"You think they wouldn't have noticed?" I began to sway, taking her with me, leading her in a sensuous rhythm across the bar floor. Relishing in the feel of her warmth all over me. "You think they wouldn't have seen us doing this and not realized that I knew this body as well as I did?"

"Maybe not." Lainie tucked her face into my neck and rested her head on my shoulder. Her body went soft and pliable, following my every move as I took us across the floor. This was not a modern sort of dance—there were no hips gyrating or grinding going on. This was slow and sensual, the sort of dance that was an appetizer of things to come later. A first kiss at the start of the night.

A wish—one that couldn't be fulfilled.

"What were you and Elijah whispering about?" I asked on a turn by the jukebox. Lainie lifted her head, but I gripped her a little tighter, keeping her hips in line with mine. Keeping her in my arms for as long as I was allowed.

"You being nosy, Deacon Manns?"

"Yes. Absolutely. Though, you can't really blame me. It's self-preservation after all."

This time, she did pull away. Not a lot. Just enough to raise her head and give me that blue stare. "Why's that?"

I leaned down, unable to resist those pink lips. Dropping a super-quick, soft kiss right in the middle of that pout.

"Because they'd all likely kill me if they knew the things I think about when you're running through my mind."

The corners of her mouth turned up, and she huffed a sort of laugh. "Neanderthals, all of you."

"Guilty as charged." I slowed the dance down even more, lessening the sway. Keeping her in my arms with our faces close. "What was the whispering about?"

"He wanted to let me know the signal."

"What signal?"

"The one I would give him if I wanted him to disappear so you and I could be alone."

Shock was an understatement. The woman—and the entire Kennard family, to be honest—never ceased to amaze me. "Does he know?"

About us. About that night. About the things we did together. About Elaine instead of Lainie. About how much I want to do it all again.

She was already shaking her head as my mind went reeling. "No, but I think he's guessing."

"Are we that obvious?"

"No, but Elijah knows me better than anyone." She lifted her shoulder in a shrug, dropping her gaze to the side. Almost as if she were looking at the floor. "He can tell I have feelings for you."

The entire bar might as well have lost its footings and slid sideways down the damn mountain for how absolutely gobsmacked I felt. Sure, I knew she found me attractive. And yeah, we had some chemistry. But feelings? Real, honest *feelings*?

I was an absolute idiot for not figuring that out sooner. "You do?"

Lainie didn't seem soothed by my response. In fact, she tugged away from me, almost as if she wanted to escape. I wasn't having it. I held her tighter, kept her pressed to me. Made sure she felt every inch of my body against hers. I stared her down until she finally got angry enough to look me square in the eye again.

Ooh, she was mad. "How can I not?"

That was all I needed to hear. I leaned in and kissed that pouty mouth again, this time not being so soft or quick. I kissed her slow and deep, groaning when she opened her mouth for me. Digging my fingers into her flesh when she rose onto the balls of her feet to move even closer. Everything about her was so soft and beautiful, so filled with life. She appealed to me in every single possible way. And I was an asshole for not telling her that.

I broke the kiss, breathing hard as I leaned my forehead against hers. "I can't do casual with you, Lainie."

The woman took my statement in stride, looking up at me with a serious expression on her beautiful face. "And I can't be second place to you behind my brothers. *Any* of my brothers."

"You're right." I swung us around, dancing with her again. "You deserve to be first place. Always."

She didn't look as if she believed me, but she let me keep holding her. Danced with me some more as I played with her hair and fought the urges within me. This woman was pure temptation—gorgeous and smart and funny and confident. How could anyone resist her? How could they expect me to?

But I had to. This time.

I sighed and stepped back, letting her go for the first time since we started our dance. "We can't do this tonight."

"What?" She came closer, nearly boxing me in against the jukebox. "What is it that we can't do tonight, Deacon?"

She was pushing me for a reaction, and I was in just the right mood to give her one. "Fuck, Lainie. We can't fuck tonight. Not unless we can figure out what to do afterward."

"You're an overthinker." She ran a finger down my chest, looking like a damn tiger about to enjoy a good meal. "Fucking is exactly what we should do. Scratch the itch one last time, you know?"

That *one last time* hurt. It really did. I reached out and yanked her against me, wrapping my arms around her waist and grabbing her by the ass to hold her to me. "You're more than just an itch, Elaine Kennard."

"Don't do that," she said, pulling away again. Putting more space between us than before. "Don't say swoony things then use my name against me."

Another sigh from me, another moment of pure and utter failure on my end. "I'm sorry."

"Fine. I'm still mad at you, though."

"I deserve that." I shook my head and headed for the bar. "I think I should take you home now."

Lainie didn't say anything, but she followed me to the bar and picked up her phone. The music suddenly stopped, the room going silent once more. Empty and quiet and...lonely. A business that reflected its owner pretty well.

Without a word, we closed up the bar and headed out. Lainie let me open the truck door for her, but she didn't whisper that polite little thank you as she had all the times before. She simply moved past me and climbed in, refusing to even look my way. If ever I had needed a sign of if I'd fucked up or not, her forgetting her manners was it. I was an idiot and an asshole, and she was giving me what I deserved.

I hated it, though.

Truck started and warm, I threw the thing into drive and rolled out. Waiting until we were on the highway heading for town before I even attempted to apologize.

"Lainie, I—"

"You told me I lit up the room."

I froze, confused. Only for a moment, though. "That night."

"Yeah, that night. You told me that's why you were so glad I came to sit by you. Because I lit up the room when you were feeling really dark."

"Still true."

"You said I made you feel alive for the first time in a long time."

I gritted my teeth, trying real hard to keep my breaths even. "Also true."

She turned in her seat, looking right at me. Pinning me in place. "What is it that's so dark and dead inside of you?"

I choked out a sarcastic sort to laugh. "You're too smart for your own good."

"No, I'm observant. It's part of my job. I've been assuming you left me alone in that hotel room because you figured out who I was and couldn't handle the fallout from my brothers, but I'm beginning to wonder if it's something else. If you don't self-sabotage your life in other ways too." She unbuckled her seat belt and rolled forward, crawling across the bench seat toward me. Moving close enough to whisper in my ear. "You fucked me like I was a lifeboat in the middle of a stormy sea but abandoned me to sink back under the waves. Why is that?"

The steering wheel creaked under my fists. "Stop it, Lainie."

She sat back in her seat, looking all sorts of proud of herself. "I threw you another life preserver tonight. You could have fucked me on your bar. Bent me over the top and had your way with me, and I would have been just as willing as before. Just as up for whatever you threw at me. You didn't take it, though."

I bit my lip, my cock hard and my leg bouncing. This woman was pure evil. "Lainie, I—"

"You just keep leaving me wanting more."

That was it. I jerked the truck onto the side of the road and slammed it into park. In one move, I threw off my seat belt, moved the whole seat back, and lunged for her. I was on her in a flash, lips meeting and tongues tangling. I didn't hold back this time—not for a second. I let my hands wander where they wanted to, let them slide up under her clothes and tug down her bra cups. I wanted to suck on those nipples so bad, wanted to taste her flesh, but between the position and the fact that I couldn't stop kissing her, I had to settle for pinching them instead. Lainie gasped and arched into my hold, her nails finding purchase on the back of my neck. I was going to have scratches for sure, not that I minded.

"Scooch down," I said, directing her to a better position. One where I could hang half off the bench. One where I could get access to more of her body. "I'm not fucking you tonight, Lainie. I told you I won't until we can figure this shit out. But I won't leave you wanting. Never that."

She stared at me, eyes all bright and wide, chest heaving, before giving me a single nod. The consent I was looking for. Without another moment wasted, I leaned up and fused my mouth with hers again, loving the sweet, chocolaty taste left there from the martini she'd drunk. A taste that was pure Lainie. I slid my hand down her chest and stomach, slipping under the waistband of her stretchy pants and into the top of her panties, focused solely on the sound of her breathing growing faster and harder.

Then I paused.

"Tell me," I mumbled against her mouth. "If you want me to stop, tell me."

She pulled me in tighter, dug those nails deeper as she whispered, "I don't want you to stop."

Consent phase two...accomplished. Onward.

I moved my mouth to her neck so I could get a taste of her flesh, needing to lower myself a little more to get the right angle for my arm. Once in a good position, I slipped my hand deeper into her panties, finding her wet and warm and so fucking soft. I nearly came right there without a single touch from her. Without seeing a bit of flesh that I wasn't supposed to. Just the feel of her body responding to mine was enough to have me groaning and wishing we were someplace else during a different time.

"I won't fuck you," I promised, biting on her neck softly. "But I'll make sure your pussy isn't needy. I'll take care of it and you, beautiful. Always."

With that, I slid two fingers inside her, nudging my way back and forth until I could glide right on in. I didn't go easy on her—it was cold, and we were on the side of the motherfucking road for anyone to come up on. I went deep and hard, pressing my thumb against her clit as I rocked my hand in and out. As I curved my fingers and rolled them against her inner flesh. Delving deep into the heat and wet I had so missed.

Lainie gasped and arched and clung to me, writhing on the seat. Fully clothed but completely debauched. There was no mistaking what was happening to her, no confusing the expression of ecstasy on her face for anything other than what it was. The woman was going to come at my hand, on my fingers. In my truck.

I almost felt like a kid all over again.

"That's it," I said as her legs began to shake. "That's my girl. Let me feel you come all over me."

Lainie groaned something that sounded like my name and reached for me, tugging me in to kiss her again. Panting against my lips as she held me. As she anchored herself to me. As she tensed and twisted and moaned long and loud as her body finally pulsed around my fingers. Minutes, hours, seconds—didn't matter. I held on and kept pushing her, not wanting this to end too soon. Not wanting her to walk away even the slightest bit unsatisfied. I kept fucking her with my hand until she squeezed her legs together and forced me to stop.

I dropped another soft, wet kiss on those pouty lips. "You're so fucking gorgeous when you come. You're also wet as fuck—I think you drowned my watch."

"You don't wear a watch." She laughed, pushing my arm away and forcing my hand out of her. "I don't think I've been finger-fucked on the side of the road since high school."

I grimaced, still clinging to her. Taking advantage of every second alone and in the dark with her. "Yeah, it's not my finest moment."

She kissed me again, softer this time. Sweeter. Smiling at me when she pulled away. "It was what we both needed."

I sighed and rested my head against hers, absorbing the affection she offered. Wishing for so much more but knowing we weren't there yet.

I was about to tell her we'd better get going, that I should take her home for the night. I was about to help her sit up and then crawl back into the driver's seat.

But the cab of the truck lit up.

The roar of an approaching engine broke the stillness of the night.

And that's when everything went to shit.

Chapter Twelve

LAINIE

I was still in the glow, still lying across the seat with Deacon practically hovering over me, when lights flashed in the rearview mirror. I jerked, my mind immediately jumping to the assumption of cops or one of my brothers or someone else from town who would know me and spread the gossip of what I'd been up to.

It was when Deacon sat up and cursed a rough *fuck* under his breath that I knew how wrong I was.

"Bad guys?" I moved to sit up, but Deacon laid a hand across my chest, holding me in place.

"Likely," he said, eyes on the mirrors and phone in his other hand. "Get on the floorboard."

"What?"

"Get on the floorboard," he said, his voice much louder and sterner than before. "Now."

I did as I was told, curling myself as best I could under the glove

121

box. No way would someone not see me if they walked up to the doors, but I was pretty well hidden from anyone driving by.

If only they had driven by.

"Lainie, I need you to follow my directions to the letter." Deacon clutched his phone in one hand and stared out the window at his side mirror, watching whatever was happening that was lighting up the inside of the truck cab. "I'm going to get out—"

"No."

"Fucking listen. I'm going to get out and deal with this. You sit tight. Don't move. I'm only leaving the driver's door unlocked. If you hear shots or I don't come back, I want you to jump into this seat and take off."

No way. Not happening. "Can't we call for help?"

"I've texted the team, but I have no idea how long it will take for them to get here. Just...stay hidden and let me handle this." He looked down at me, his face stoic and his eyes hard. An expression I didn't recognize. "If my phone goes off, answer it. If they text back, send them answers to whatever they need to know." He handed me his phone, not looking away. "Code's ten-twenty-six."

Ten-twenty-six. Two days before Alder's wedding. The night we...

"Deacon..."

"Don't get sentimental on me now, beautiful. I'm busy keeping you alive." With that, he pulled a handgun from the console and opened his door. "Stay put unless you need to get the fuck out of here. Got it?"

"Yeah." I gripped his phone to my chest, hanging on to that lifeline as if it were my only chance for survival. It very likely was.

DEACON

I stepped out of my truck and into the cold, night air with my entire body on high alert. Four bikes sat behind my truck, three with riders on them. The fourth guy had dismounted and stood off to the side. Watching. Likely the scout—armed and ready to take out me or anyone else seen as a threat. A great setup, and one that told me they'd planned this. They'd known exactly what to do once they had me pulled over.

I'd made it easy on them by being a sitting duck on the side of the road. And not alone, too.

This was bad—real fucking bad. Getting caught up with the Soul Suckers alone would have been one thing, but I had Lainie with me. Had the evidence of her presence on my hand still. I had to keep the fuckers away from the cab of my truck—and her—no matter what.

"Barkeep!" a man yelled as I reached the back end of my truck. "It's nice to see you."

I leaned a hip against the bumper and crossed one ankle over the other, playing the calm and casual game. "Sorry, can't say the same. Y'all lost or something?"

The man on the lead bike, obviously the mouthpiece of the group, flicked his headlamp off and leaned forward. "I've got a boss who'd like to talk to you. Figured we'd come and issue an invitation."

"An invitation. On the side of the road." I nodded, pretending to think it over for a second. "Sorry, but I'm busy."

"Didn't tell you when he wanted to talk to you."

"Don't need to. I'm busy."

Mouthpiece's smile never even slipped. "You're going to want to talk to this guy. He'll make it worth your while."

My doubts were high on that. "Yeah, well, you're not getting me tonight. Want to set up a meeting? Send me an actual invitation. Preferably letterpress on that thick, fancy paper they use for weddings. We can meet at the Applebee's out in Stickley."

"Didn't picture you for an Applebee's man."

"Their bourbon options suck ass, but they've got good appetizers. I'm a sucker for onion rings."

Mouthpiece laughed. "You're really turning us down?"

"I sure the fuck am. But hey, like I said, send a man an invitation, and I might show up."

He shook his head, still grinning. "I'd heard some stories about you, barkeep. Looks like you're living up to the hype."

"Don't believe everything you hear." Though, being that they were Soul Suckers, and that I'd helped Chase take out a few of their own along with some powerful Black Angels club members, they might have solid info on me. Not that I was going to confirm or deny a damn thing. Not with Lainie so fucking close to me. Alder and the guys needed to haul a little ass. My good nature wouldn't last forever.

Leader guy never stopped smiling my way. The look on his face, the stare, was downright creepy in its intensity. He knew something good. Or at least thought he did.

And he played his hand like a champ. "You planning on trying to hide, Sniper?"

My gut turned to ice and my muscles locked into place, though I kept my face as bland as possible. He could have called me Sniper because he knew what my job in the military was—that was something I never tried to hide. I doubted that, though. See, I'd given myself a nickname when dealing with a Black Angels bigwig. One we ended up taking out, but I had a feeling that dude wasn't going to come up. This was a Soul Suckers crew, which meant—

"Maybe you remember some friends of mine," he said, still

smiling my way. Looking more and more snakelike in the shadows. "Grudge and Bama. Recognize those names, Sniper?"

Fuck me. I sure as hell did. I also knew why I'd been asked to take them out.

"Can't say I do. You say you were friends with them? What kind? Like drinking buddies or long-term? You meet them when you were just kids?"

The man sat back, his smile turning into a scowl. Yeah, I'd hit the nerve. Grudge and Bama had been Soul Suckers who were involved in human trafficking of little kids, one of which had been related to a Black Angels leader. I'd traded taking out the two perverts to gain Jinx's freedom from the club. So yeah, I'd killed two of theirs—ones who'd deserved death. And if Mouthpiece's response to my using the word kids was any indication, he'd known about their predilections. He may have even been involved. I'd never claimed to be a good guy, but in my world, you didn't fuck with kids. Ever. They were off-limits to the extreme. These bastards didn't follow the same rules, which meant they were garbage. Human garbage.

And it looked like they'd come to seek a little vengeance on me because I'd been the one to take out the trash.

"Anyway," I said, focusing on my hands as I picked at a hangnail. Refusing to give in to their little show of force. "It's too cold out here to be chatting about people I don't know. If y'all are done—"

"Who you got in the truck with you?"

I broke. I couldn't help it. I darted my eyes to the man who'd spoken—the one standing off to the side—and I took half a step forward before I even realized I'd moved. No way. No fucking way were they getting any information on Lainie from me.

"You don't want to play that game with me, son."

Standing guy didn't move or speak. He simply kept staring me down with an expression on his face that told me he at least thought he held the power in the situation. And maybe he did—they'd found me alone with Lainie on the side of a dark and deserted stretch of highway. Maybe their four-to-one fighting style would have worked just fine if the darkness hadn't been squashed at that moment by a pair of headlights coming at them from behind me. I saw Mouthpiece's mouth fall open, saw the headlamps light up his face. Their advantage had just dropped considerably.

The cavalry had arrived.

Mouthpiece wasn't done with me, though. "This ain't over."

"Yeah, it is." I pushed off the side of the truck as Gage sidled up beside me. Another truck appeared from behind the bikers, lights blaring through the darkness. They were surrounded. "Get the fuck out of our town."

"Or what?"

Bishop—hanging out the driver's side door of his truck with a rifle on his shoulder—answered that question for me. "Or you die, motherfuckers. It's not that hard to figure out."

Gage snorted a laugh at my side, obviously entertained by his partner.

I could only shrug. "You heard the man."

The standing biker returned to his ride, settling astride it and starting the engine. The others followed his lead, engines firing all over. A sick sense of realization landed squarely on my head—I'd been wrong. Mouthpiece hadn't been the leader, and the guy standing hadn't been the guard. They'd played me so I paid attention to the person they wanted me to, not to the one I should have been watching. Fuck me, I almost had to respect the game they'd just played. Almost.

As the bikers turned to pull out onto the highway, the one who'd been standing—the actual leader of the crew—caught my attention once more.

"You're good, barkeep. But you're not the only sniper around these parts. I'll be keeping an eye on you."

And with that, he rolled off with the other three following him. I stood on the side of the road, Gage with me, both of us watching them leave.

It was Gage who broke the silence. "You okay?"

"No. Not in the least."

"She okay?"

Lainie. Who was still in the truck waiting for me. "She'd better be."

"Make sure, then follow me to town. Bishop's got your six, and I'll shoot Alder a message to meet us there."

"Thanks," I said, taking one moment to fill my lungs with air and blow it back out. Then I was in motion, wanting to check on Lainie. Needing to see her face. Which happened a lot sooner than I expected as, when I opened the door to my truck, she was halfway up the seat instead of on the floorboard where I'd told her to stay.

I loved that woman, even if she never could do what she was told.

"You just couldn't follow the rules, could you?"

Chapter Thirteen

LAINIE

Engines rumbled outside and lights shone through the windows above, but my little space was insulated from all that a bit. Almost too insulated. I had no idea how much time had passed or what was going on outside. All I knew was my entire body felt as if it were on some sort of red alert—attentive, focused, and definitely ready to do something other than hide.

The phone vibrated, making me jump and bump my head on the dash. My hands shook so much that I nearly dropped the thing trying to unlock it and tap to see what was on the screen. Thankfully, I was able to hold on and get to what I needed.

Gage: Three minutes out.

"Three minutes. Okay. Just three minutes." I entered the passcode and tapped to open the messaging app. His entire phone ran in dark mode, making it not emit as much light as if he'd been in light mode. Smart on his part because I didn't worry too much about someone outside the truck seeing the light from the screen. I pulled up the thread and took a quick look at the messages.

Deacon had sent them an SOS that the Soul Suckers had the two of us pulled over. They knew I was with him, at least.

Another reply popped up as I was staring at the screen.

Alder: Keep Lainie safe. I'm coming.

My heart melted a little. Alder being Alder—protective as ever. I hurried up and sent a note back to the thread.

I'm hiding in the truck. Deacon is outside dealing with whoever is out there. HURRY. -L

I hugged the phone to my chest and waited. My head started to hurt from the pressure of trying to listen for anything. The rumbles had ceased and I could hear the occasional hum of what I assumed were men talking, but otherwise, it was just me and the blood pounding through my body. Gage had said three minutes, so I started counting to keep a relatively solid grasp of time passing.

I had made it to sixty-seven seconds when I finally had the urge to say *fuck it*. Knowing this was likely going to make Deacon mad, I slithered up the seat and tucked myself against the back of it. I tugged my hair back, not wanting the pale color to reflect or pick up any light, and peeked over the edge toward the rear window.

Four bikes. I could see four bikes with their headlights shining. I crouched down again and unlocked Deacon's phone, reopening the thread.

I see four motorcycles behind the truck. Can't see Deacon.

Once done, I set the phone down and crept across the seat, staying low. I was halfway across the driver's seat when I was finally able to see anything in the mirror. Deacon stood at the very back of his truck, leaning against the end of it. As far away from me as he could get and yet still close, too. Smart man. His body language seemed casual enough, but there were three men facing him, backlit from the motorcycle lights. Three men. But four bikes.

"Shit."

I dropped down again and slid across the bench, looking out the passenger's side window to see the mirror. Nothing there. Wherever number four was, he wasn't sneaking up on me. At least, I didn't think so.

Breathing hard, still not knowing what to do, I moved to slide across to the driver's side again. The windshield suddenly lit up, and the roar of an engine broke the strange and pressured silence of the cab. Outside, there was yelling—a lot of yelling. I caught a big, bearded shadow walking by the window from the front of the truck toward the back—Gage, I assumed—before another roar sounded from outside. Another vehicle. I was halfway to sitting up so I could see outside, when the driver's door opened and I was met with the very pale, very worried face of Deacon Manns. A face that still broke out into a small smile when he locked eyes with me.

"You just couldn't follow the rules, could you?" He waved his hand, indicating I should move to my seat. "Stay down, though."

I did as I was told, lying across the seat as he threw the truck in gear and peeled out. Shaking, still unclear as to what was happening, I reached out and set my hand on his thigh. He covered mine with his own, bringing it to his lips to kiss my fingers.

"You okay, beautiful?"

I snorted a very unladylike laugh. "I'm groovy. Are *you* okay?"

"Not in the fucking least, but Gage and Bishop are following us to town, and Alder is meeting us over there. You'll be safe in just a few minutes."

I gripped his thigh harder then wove our fingers together. "I'm safe with you."

He sighed, hanging on to my hand tight. "I was questioning that for a few minutes there."

"What did they want?"

"Me."

"You?"

"Yeah, me." He made a turn that forced him to release my hand then slowed down. "We'll talk about it with Alder. You're home."

I sat up, taking in the view of a very dark and quiet Main Street. For the first time in my life, the visage seemed ominous to me instead of safe. The shadows hiding potential threats instead of bathing the storefronts in sleepy peace.

Justice had changed for me.

"Deacon."

He stopped, hand on the door as if ready to open it, and turned my way. "Yeah?"

I scanned outside again, knowing Alder was parked beside us on my side, that Gage's truck rested on Deacon's, and that a third—assumably Bishop's—was behind us. I was surrounded by big, burly men who would definitely protect me, but out there was danger.

"I don't know if I can step outside."

Deacon furrowed his brow, but then something like realization slid across his handsome face. He grabbed my hand and tugged me into his side, taking me with him as he opened his door.

"I've got you, Lainie. No one is going to get that close to you again."

He pulled me after him, helping me down and wrapping an arm around me as I wobbled on my feet. Alder came rushing over from the front of the truck, looking positively thunderous.

"What the fuck was she doing out on the road with you?"

I opened my mouth to answer, but Deacon beat me to it.

"I was bringing her home. Elijah went with Zane to capture more drone footage, and I thought she'd be safe with me."

"You okay, Lainie?" Bishop asked, slipping in beside Deacon.

I nodded, hanging on to Deacon like a lifeline. "I'm fine. Deacon kept me hidden and safe."

Alder didn't seem convinced. "Let's get you inside so you don't become a target."

"What? No. I thought—"

"Inside," Alder barked, heading for the alley that would lead us to the door to access the apartments over the hardware store. "We can talk upstairs."

Deacon patted my arm and pulled me with him, not letting go for a second. We all made it upstairs and into the apartment—well, all but Gage. He took a guarding position at the bottom of the stairs and stayed put. Alder, Deacon, and Bishop followed me inside, though. Deacon let me go to walk in alone, not that I was happy about that.

Even my apartment didn't seem as light and airy as before.

"First things first," Alder said, pacing the small living area. "You're canceling your girls' night."

I hadn't even thought about that, about the plans to go out and have fun with Katie, Mercy, and Shye. Katie had said we'd need a chaperone—I'd had one with Deacon tonight, and we'd still gotten stopped. Still needed to call for help because we were outnumbered.

This wasn't one I was going to fight about. "Fine."

Alder watched me, stoic expression on his face. As if waiting for more of an answer. He wouldn't be getting one. Tonight had taught me a rough lesson in the safety of Justice, or lack thereof.

"It shouldn't be so cold up here." I wrapped my arms around

myself, trying to control the trembling that seemed to be taking over my body. "Anyone want a coffee or something?"

"No, thank you," Deacon said, giving me a sad little smile. "I think you need something to warm you up, though."

"Adrenaline crash." Bishop headed into the kitchen, opening cabinet doors and pulling out a box of something I hadn't even seen in there. "Tea. Anabeth always drinks this stuff before bed. It's got some sort of flower in it to help you sleep."

"Chamomile?" Deacon asked.

Bishop squinted at the box. "Yeah. That shit." He filled a pot with water and put it on the stove, digging out a mug and adding hot water from the tap to it. "She usually puts honey in it, but I don't see any. Sugar okay?"

I shrugged. "That's fine."

We stood around in silence as Bishop—big, brash, loud brother of mine—made me a cup of tea like I was some sort of royal figure and he was a butler. It was disconcerting, to be honest.

"Here," he said once the bag was in the cup and hot water covered it. "The box said to steep it for three minutes, but it might be good to sip on now."

I settled onto a barstool at the counter and took hold of the cup, cradling it to warm my hands. "I didn't know you were a tea guy."

He grunted. "I'm not, but my wife is a tea woman, and I work really fucking hard to keep her happy."

I nodded toward him, raising my cup in mock salute. "Good man."

"Speaking of men," Alder said, breaking the calm vibe we'd developed. "What the fuck happened out there?"

I glanced at Deacon, who seemed super tense. He avoided my gaze.

"Zane, Elijah, Lainie, and I met at the bar to talk about what we'd seen in the woods—"

Alder interrupted him. "The man with the binoculars."

"Right. Elijah and Zane wanted to get more footage before nightfall to see if there was a secondary camp, so they left, and I agreed to take Lainie home. We were on our way here when the bikers showed up behind me."

"Why didn't you just keep driving?" Bishop asked. "We would have met up with you."

I caught a slight flinch from Deacon, met his eyes for the briefest of moments before refocusing on my mug of tea.

"We were already pulled over."

"Why?" Alder asked, his voice gruff and mean. Soldier-mode, activated.

Well, he wasn't the only Kennard who knew how to play a role. "I was sick to my stomach."

Three sets of eyes turned my way, the attention making my gut actually ache and clench a little. *In for a penny, in for a pound.*

I shrugged and lifted my mug of tea, trying to sound as casual as possible. "I'm about to start my period and was crampy. I thought I was going to throw up, so Deacon pulled over."

Bishop and Alder looked away, their faces twisting slightly. They fit the pattern—talk about menstruating around men and they get grossed out and uncomfortable. Deacon...well, he stared straight at me, his lips turning up the tiniest bit. Almost smiling. I had a feeling he liked that response.

"Okay, so you pulled over," Alder said, totally skipping the part about why. I took that as a win.

Deacon slid his gaze my way one more time before refocusing on my brother. "Right. While we were on the side of the road, four bikes rolled up on me. I told Lainie to hide under the dash as much as possible and got out to deal with them."

Alder nodded, beginning to pace the length of the kitchen. "Good call. Her presence would have added tension to the moment."

"Exactly."

"What did they want?" Bishop asked, leaning on the counter beside me. He also leaned down to whisper, "Need more tea?"

I smiled up at him, shaking my head.

"They wanted me to come meet with the head of their club."

Alder stopped pacing, frowning. "Why you?"

Deacon shrugged. "No clue, but that's what they wanted. And what they still want—a meeting with me and this club leader guy."

"What did you tell them?"

"That I wouldn't come with them tonight, but that we could work something out."

Alder nodded. "Good. Okay, good. Yeah. We should plan something out. Set up a meeting and—"

"Blow them the fuck off the earth?" Bishop shrugged when I spun to gape at him. "It's a SEAL thing."

Alder rolled his eyes. "Not blow them up. Not yet." He shook his head and strode for the door. "Okay, I need to get home to Shye. Let's reconvene in the morning and figure something out. I don't like this."

Bishop gave my shoulder a rub before rising to his feet and following our brother. "Sounds good. Lainie, you call us if you need anything, okay?"

"Of course." I gripped my mug harder, my pulse quickening. "I'll be fine."

Deacon stared at me long and hard, likely hearing the quaver in my voice, possibly knowing how much of a lie that was. He didn't say anything, though. Instead, he walked out with the guys and shut the door behind himself. Leaving me alone.

All. Alone.

I was up and on my feet in seconds, engaging every lock on the door. Poor Elijah was going to have to wake me up if he wanted in once I went to bed, but that was his problem. If he'd have been there, I wouldn't have been so nervous. If he'd have come home... *I should text him. Find out where he is.*

I had just picked up my phone when it rang, the vibration and noise nearly making me drop the thing. It wasn't Elijah's info on my screen, though.

The second the call connected, Deacon asked, "You okay, beautiful?"

I sighed, my body relaxing slightly at the sound of his voice. "Not completely, but I'm working on it."

"Yeah, I figured. Tonight's activities put a lot of stress on you."

"Activities. Do you mean the dancing, the finger-banging, or the Soul Suckers tracking us down?"

He chuckled low and quiet. "All three."

I sighed and moved into the living room, settling onto the couch and covering myself with a blanket. "Yeah, well, it was. All three. But I'm fine."

"Bad answer. Fine is too generic for you."

"Pushy bastard."

"Always. So how are you, really?"

I sat still and silent for a long moment, letting my brain truly focus on that question. Searching for the right answer.

"I'm suddenly afraid of Justice."

"You can go home, you know. Back to Denver."

As much as I would have thought that might have been the right thing to do, it felt wrong. "Not yet. I'm not ready to give up just yet."

Deacon stayed quiet for a long moment, both of us simply breathing on the phone. There was no noise. No engine or road sounds, something that took me way longer to realize than it should have.

"Where are you?" I asked, sitting up a little straighter. Already knowing the answer but not wanting to get my hopes up.

"Look out your front window."

I jumped to my feet and rushed across the room, peeking past the curtains to look outside. Deacon's truck sat on Main Street, lights off. He had stayed.

"You get guard duty tonight?"

"I volunteered."

"Why?"

"Because I wanted to make sure you were okay. Are you okay?"

"I'd be better if I weren't alone."

"You're not alone. I'm right here."

"I'd like it better if you were up here with me."

"Ah, beautiful. I would, but that could lead to funny business."

"I like funny business with you."

He chuckled all low and gravelly. "And I like funny business with you, but I need to play tonight straight. I don't want those bikers getting that close to you again."

"Fine. But I'm lodging a complaint."

"What kind of complaint?"

"The kind of complaint that comes from having a really good orgasm and not being able to return the favor."

"Shouldn't that be my complaint?"

"What can I say? I'm a giver."

"You're trouble is what you are."

"Don't I know it."

He laughed again, the sound cutting off when I yawned. "You tired, beautiful?"

"Yeah. I think that tea Bishop made for me is working."

"So, go to bed."

I gripped the edge of the curtain harder. "I'm not ready to hang up yet."

"Then don't." He grunted, obviously moving around. "There. I'm lying down on the seat. You go lie down on your bed, and we'll keep talking."

I pressed a finger against the glass, the cold shooting all the way up my arm and making me shiver. "Promise?"

"I'm not going anywhere, Lainie. Go get ready for bed, and I'll be here."

"Okay." I was halfway across the room, leaving lights on because the idea of sitting in the dark made my heart jump, when I finally said, "Thank you, Deacon. For everything."

"Anything for you. Now, get your pajamas on. And hey, let a guy know when you're naked so I can follow along in my head."

"Who says I wear pajamas?"

He groaned long and loud. "Well, fuck me sideways, never thought I'd be ready to jack off right here on Main Street for all the town to see."

"You're an animal."

"Woof." He chuckled again then said, "Go to bed, beautiful. No one will be getting any closer to you than I am right now."

And somehow, I believed him.

Chapter Fourteen

DEACON

Fucked. Everything about my life was fucked. I had a motorcycle club wanting to meet with me, had Alder's little sister on my mind in the naughtiest of ways, and had a crick in my back and neck from sleeping in the cab of my truck. I had woken up in a foul mood and was likely to stay in it all day. Mostly because of how my night had been upended twice over, both times due to Lainie. Which meant dealing with Alder this morning was going to be loads of fun.

I owed that man my life ten times over, and fucking his little sister was not the way to pay him back.

But Lainie...*Elaine.*

"I need some fucking coffee," I mumbled to myself as I parked in Alder's driveway, hoping like hell Shye was about to be her usual hostess self and offer me some when she saw me. Hell, at that point, I was willing to ring the doorbell and ask for some. It had been a long night.

A long night with Lainie in my ear for most of it, either chatting or simply breathing. Second-best night of my adult life, for sure. I hadn't been kidding her when I'd said I'd need to put a ring on her finger for Alder to accept us, though. I wasn't even sure that would be enough for the man. He still saw her as a child. Not that marrying the woman was a realistic option—Alder would still kick my ass, and she'd likely run the second I brought it up as a possibility. She'd accepted me joking about it, but I had a feeling if I got serious...

If I truly asked her...

She'd be gone.

And Alder would *still* be mad at me.

My entire world was one large dilemma.

"Seriously," I huffed as I stepped out of the truck. "Need coffee."

"Deacon?" The angel herself had opened the door to the house and stood leaning halfway onto the porch. She looked a little tired and pale but still had a big smile on her face. "I've got a fresh pot of coffee on if you'd like a cup."

Praise be. "You are a queen among peasants, and I will accept that coffee with much gratitude."

Shye giggled and waved me inside. I followed her through the door, sticking to the landing by the door to give the woman some space. She really did seem pale, the skin under her eyes almost blue-toned.

"You good, Shye? Everything okay here?"

Shye lifted her shoulders in a delicate shrug. "Of course. Everything's fine."

Fine. I truly hated when women used that word. It was a definite sign that things were not in any way fine.

"You let me know if you need help keeping Alder in line. I'm not afraid to go head-to-head with the jackass."

"Who's a jackass?" Alder himself walked down the stairs, looking fresh and recently showered. "Morning, Deac."

"Morning. Your lovely bride was just making me a cup of coffee."

His face twisted, concern appearing. "You sure you're—"

"I'm fine." Shye gave him a stiff smile, relaxing it as she turned to me. "You brutes are overprotective. Here's your coffee—let me know if you need more."

She handed me a travel mug—a big one. There had to be a good twenty ounces of hot, brewed heaven inside it.

"I think I'm in love," I said just before I took a sip. Shooting sweet Shye a wink over the edge of the mug for good measure. She grinned and waved me off just like normal, but I still didn't like the lack of color in her cheeks. It was when she yawned, nearly doubling over at the effort, that I took a good, long look at my best friend. "Everything okay, boss?"

"Yeah." Alder hurried into the kitchen area, wrapping his arms around Shye and giving her a soft kiss on the head. "It was a late night around here."

I took another sip of coffee, raising my eyebrows over the edge. It was a late night everywhere, apparently. "Anything I can help with?"

"Pretty sure they're both tired because of me."

I spun and nearly dropped my mug of necessary brain fuel. I obviously hadn't drunk enough of it yet because I could have sworn one Camden Reese—widower, first in town to lose someone to the Soul Suckers, and man who'd been following one hell of a destructive path when he left—was standing on the stairs.

Alder responded first. "Yeah, as you can see, Camden's home. He showed up last night and needed a place to stay."

Which meant they were both up late, making sure their guest felt at home. And likely getting as much information as possible on where he'd been and what he'd been doing. Last I'd seen the man, he'd been a freight train of pain rolling toward a death fueled by alcoholism and hate.

He didn't look anything like that this morning.

In fact, he looked clean-cut, wide awake, and about as pre-Leah-death as I'd ever seen him. Had I somehow walked into an alternate universe?

The man who had once kept me up at night as I wondered if he was alive or not gave me a smile and held out his fist for a bump. "Good to see you, Deacon."

And then the fucker smiled. He *smiled*.

"I'm going to need way more coffee for this."

* * *

Once everyone had drunk some coffee and Alder had successfully shooed Shye back to bed to get some rest, we headed to the barn. We being me, Alder, and Camden. Apparently, Gage, Bishop, and even Zane were already there and waiting on us. It was a motherfucking party that I was simply not in the mood for.

"We take them out." Bishop greeted us with an order, rising to his feet the second we walked through the door. "Now. Immediately. None of this fucking diplomacy and subterfuge shit."

"So," I said, crossing the space toward Zane, while the rest of the group converged behind me. "It's going to be *that* kind of morning."

Bishop wasn't finished, though. "They could have killed you, Deac. Lainie, too. Last night was the final straw. They need to go. Wait... Camden? When did you get home?"

I left the men to their welcoming, finding the lone wolf of the group—Undersheriff Zane Grogan—and planting myself to his side. We stood quiet and watchful as the conversation across the barn went from welcome home to kill them all.

"You ever get the feeling we keep having the same conversation in different formats?" Zane asked, watching the rest of the men. "Didn't we already settle on not committing first-degree murder?"

I shrugged, drinking my coffee and giving my brain time to wake the fuck up. As Alder and Bishop argued back and forth about whether to kill people or not, Elijah slipped in through the door. Seeing him there—unshaven and rumpled but awake—jogged loose a memory from the night before. Actually, from just a couple hours before. Early morning. I leaned closer to Zane and lowered my voice.

"You and Elijah had a late night. He go to bible study with you?"

He didn't react, though his voice sounded a little tight as he said, "I don't know what you're talking about."

"Really? Huh. I just assumed he was with you. See, I was parked outside their apartment all night and didn't see the man until about four this morning. But perhaps I was wrong and he was just...out. In the woods. Alone." I took a sip of my coffee and leaned against the stall wall behind me. "He definitely seems the type to do some solo winter hiking."

"But let none of you suffer as a murderer or a thief or an evildoer —" he shot me a glare "—or as a meddler."

I couldn't hold back my grin. "Bible verses, murder plots, and coffee. It's my kind of morning."

It was as Bishop circled around to make his argument for full destruction for the third time that the coffee kicked in.

"I'm going to talk to them."

Every man in the room turned my way, all silent and staring as if I had just said I'd grown a second dick.

"You're going to *what?*" Alder asked. "Why?"

I shrugged and took another sip of coffee, knowing this wouldn't go over well with the death and destruction twins. "Last night, they said they have a leader who wants to talk to me. Not Alder, not a Kennard—me. There has to be a reason for that. I want to know what the reason is."

Alder seemed positively gobsmacked. "We don't *talk* to the enemy."

And see, that was where he was wrong. Really fucking wrong. "Pretty sure I learned three different languages just to be able to talk to our enemies, boss."

"That was different."

"No, that's the exact same. Except this time, the enemy is close to your family, so you're seeing the attack through a personal lens." I pushed off the wall, keeping my eyes on his. Knowing I was likely pushing him too far. "We have to understand them to get a grasp on their endgame. We can't just start murdering people randomly."

"It's self-defense," Bishop said, sounding far angrier and more upset than I'd been prepared for. "They've already killed some of our own. We can't just set up Justice residents like a goddamned buffet for the wolf."

Elijah piped up for the first time. "That's not self-defense. Legally, unless there's an immediate threat, you can't be the aggressor without facing charges. The Soul Suckers just being in town would not be considered an immediate threat."

Zane backed up his friend. "The lawyer's right. We're crossing a line here."

Gage huffed. "Tell that to Camden."

The room went quiet and still again, this time, all eyes focusing on the man of the hour. The prodigal son who'd only just returned. The one who'd already lost far too much.

Camden didn't even flinch. "I'm here for one man and only one. What you all decide to do with the rest of the Soul Suckers is on you, but Coyote dies. I'll face murder charges if I have to."

I caught Zane looking my way out of the corner of my eye, but I couldn't look away from the image before me. Camden was...not himself. His voice was flat, his eyes dead. He looked like a younger, healthier version on the outside, but inside...zombie.

Fuck me, he was going to be like a rabid stray dog running around town. This was not what we needed.

"We're not doing this," I said, knowing I needed to lock down Bishop and Gage before they fed into Camden's thinking and we had three loose cannons. "I'm going to talk to them first. I'll handle it."

"Handle what, exactly?" Alder said, crossing his arms and glaring my way.

"The communication piece. If meeting up with them seems dangerous or if anything happens, go forth into full SEAL mode with my blessing and understanding. But I'm not a SEAL, and I don't roll that way. Not yet, at least."

"I'm with Deacon," Elijah said, moving to stand beside me in a physical representation of his support. "Talk first, kill later."

Zane took his spot on my other side. "Agreed. Give us twenty-four hours to try diplomacy."

Alder sighed, looking over the group one man at a time. "Fine. But if you die—" he pointed a finger my way "—I'm going to revive you, kick your ass, then let them kill you again."

As was expected. "Understood."

"I need some fucking whiskey," he said, shaking his head. "You've got one day. But if anything happens—if they get aggressive with *anyone* in town—they're done for. And if they get anywhere near my baby sister again—"

"They all die," I said, my voice a low growl I hadn't been expecting.

Alder didn't seem to notice, or he assumed I was simply on the same page as him. "Exactly. Now, let's go have some breakfast."

The group of us headed outside and for the house, breaking off into smaller pods. Bishop and Gage followed right behind Alder, neither man looking happy. Camden trailed behind them. I stuck with Elijah and Zane, knowing we'd need to have a conversation about planning out what was to happen later that day.

That day. I had one day to plan, recon, and meet with the enemy. I was so fucked.

Speaking of being fucked...

"Well, hello, sister mine," Elijah hollered. I looked up to find Lainie walking toward us, looking so fucking beautiful it hurt. The woman wore a dress—long and flowy with little flowers on it. Far too summery for the weather we were having but absolutely gorgeous on her tall frame. Also, easy access for when I tried to get between those legs again.

So not what I needed to be thinking about.

"Gentlemen," she said, eyeing every one of us in turn. It seemed like she gave me a longer look than the rest, though that could have been wishful thinking.

"It's still early," Elijah said, smiling at his sister. "You could have at least brought a pot of coffee with you."

Lainie rolled her eyes. "I'm a graduate of Colorado University with a master's in business administration focusing on communications and marketing. I'm not a server."

Alder huffed a laugh. "Old Deacon's got two bachelor's, a master's in something to do with mental health counseling, and an MBA, yet he's happy to serve me whiskey."

"I don't know if happy's the way I'd describe it." I caught Lainie's eye, a sinking feeling developing in my gut at the anger I saw there. I shrugged. "I had a lot of downtime during my service, and internet schools were just becoming a thing. But then I followed your freeloading brother out here, and the rest is Jury Room history."

"I'm not a freeloader," Alder said. "You never let me pay."

"Very true." And I never would. Some debts stuck around longer than others.

As everyone began to filter into the house, I lingered outside. Lainie lingered right along with me. Both of us dancing around the group until everyone else was simply gone.

Until I was once again alone with my favorite temptress.

"Morning, beautiful."

"Why doesn't Alder pay?"

Not the question I was expecting. "Because I owe him."

"For what?

"I told you—he saved my life."

"During your time in the military, right?"

"Yes, but I owe him not just for our time spent in the military. Afterward, too. My debt to him is bigger than normal military brotherhood."

"Big enough for you to waste your education."

That...pissed me off a little. "I own a business, Lainie. Maybe I'm not using my counseling degree, but I still offer therapy in a more convenient and palatable form. Plus, it's free. I use my MBA to make sure the bar and other businesses in town stay profitable." I leaned against the railing of the porch, looking her square in the eye. "You should think about doing the same."

"Opening a bar?"

"No. Coming home. Using your skills to help the mill grow. Help the town grow. There are plenty of empty storefronts on Main Street—bet you could think of a few ways to utilize them."

"Work for the big boss?" She scoffed but showed her hand when she looked down at the ground. "He'd probably ignore all my ideas as too immature."

"Maybe at first, but you certainly don't seem like someone who backs down from a challenge."

Her head popped up, and those blue eyes met mine again. "I get what I want."

I went from relaxed and calm to hard as a rock in a second. That look, the fire in her eyes, she wasn't talking business anymore.

Neither was I.

"Tell me, then." I stepped closer, lowering my voice. Wishing I could get my hands on her skin. "What is it you want, Lainie?"

"I want to help."

"Help what?"

"Help you guys with whatever you're planning. Alder would never let me because he's a sexist prick who thinks women can't play hardball. But I heard you—you're going to meet with the bikers. I'm an excellent negotiator and have solid intuition about people. I can be an asset."

Fuck me, the woman was brilliant. And deadly. "Alder would kill me if I let you in on this...project."

She let out a breath, her shoulders sagging. "Yeah, I guess—"

"So, let's keep this between us, okay?"

Lainie jerked back, staring hard. Looking completely shocked. "You'll let me help?"

"Of course. I'm not a sexist prick." I leaned a little closer, running my fingers over the side of her hand. Unable to resist touching her for another second. "Neither is your brother, but I have a feeling getting you to see that is going to take a fuckton of work."

Her eyes burned right into mine, defiant as ever. The woman was stronger than I could have imagined and so much more than Alder had ever given her credit for. Building her up, supporting her and surprising her, was so much fun.

"So, what's next?" she asked.

I wanted to say we go back to my place and get naked. I wanted to tell her my goal was to see what was happening under that pretty dress. I wanted so much to lose myself in her.

But I had twenty-four hours to deal with the Soul Suckers before my friends went on a murderous rampage.

Getting Lainie naked was going to have to wait.

"Let's grab Elijah and Zane so I can relegate a few jobs their way. We've got criminals to meet with."

Her grin could have set the tree line on fire. "Let me just say goodbye to Shye."

Chapter Fifteen

LAINIE

Are you sure you've got all of this?" I looked around Shye's kitchen, almost feeling guilty about leaving her alone with the plethora of pies she had planned to make. Almost, because I didn't cook. Elijah had driven me to Alder's place but left to go have fun with the boys in the barn. I'd been instructed by my eldest brother to check on his wife. She'd been...busy.

"I'm sure," Shye said, rolling even more pie crust. There were already nine pies in various stages of creation on the island. "You go with your brothers. Alder would like that."

He wouldn't, but I wasn't about to be the one to burst her Alder bubble. Still, I was hesitant to leave. The woman looked...not well.

"Shye," I said, demanding and receiving her full attention. "Are you okay? You look a little pale."

She blinked, her face completely devoid of emotion. "I'm fine."

Deacon's words wafted through my memories. *Fine is too generic.*

The woman wasn't fine, but she certainly wasn't opening up to me. Understood—I barely knew her. Still...

"You just call me if you need help tonight or tomorrow, okay? You don't have to take on this whole meal all by yourself."

She shook her head, back to rolling out pie crust. "I'm *fine.* You all keep worrying about me when there's nothing wrong. Now, go on —I love having you here, but you've got other things to do."

I nodded and headed for the door. She was right. I did have other things to do. Apparently, I was running an errand with Elijah, Zane, and Deacon. My Justice crew.

"We worry, Shye. That's all. But if you're fine, then I'm going to head out."

She nodded, completely focused on her bar of pies. I took that as acceptance and headed for the door, grabbing my coat on the way. Deacon stood on the porch waiting for me. Just Deacon.

"Where are Elijah and Zane?"

"They're making a loop of town for your brother before meeting us at the bar." He led the way toward his truck, approaching the passenger's side. "I said I'd cart your ass around for the morning."

Charmer. "Just my ass?"

He chuckled as he opened the door for me. "It's a phenomenal ass. It deserves to be the star of the show sometimes."

I grinned. Couldn't help myself. I also hopped into the truck and reached for my seat belt. Deacon jogged around the front then joined me on the seat, cranking the engine.

"So, I need you to promise me something."

I turned his way, my brow tightening. My reply coming out in a long, exaggerated sort of way. "Okay."

"Don't just agree—you don't even know what it is."

"You won't hurt me or do anything to humiliate me, so it doesn't matter. If you need a promise from me, you've got it."

He glanced my way as he waited at the bottom of the drive to turn onto the main road, those green eyes once again burning into me. There were moments when his handsomeness struck me over the head like a heavy frying pan. The eyes, the shaggy hair, the slight wrinkles from smiling. He was older than me by more than most people would accept, but he was gorgeous. He also treated me with a kindness that most men didn't grasp. Sure, he'd run after our... entanglement. I couldn't blame him, really. If I'd been honest about who I was, we wouldn't have gotten into that situation. That was more my fault. Not that I was quite ready to admit that yet.

But anyway, yeah. I didn't care about his age. I did care that his stare could make you want to confess every sin you'd ever committed, though.

"Why are you looking at me like that?"

He sat up straighter as if he hadn't realized he'd been staring. "Sorry. Sometimes I forget how fucking amazing you are."

Yeah. Age didn't matter a bit.

"Anyway," he said, refocusing on the road and turning onto the highway. "The place I'm taking you is a secret."

"Secret to whom?"

"Everyone."

"You have secrets from Alder? Shocking."

Deacon huffed a laugh. "He knows I own the place, but he's never been there. I don't like the idea of anyone else's energy messing with the vibe I've created at the cabin."

Ah, so he had a cabin in the woods. Likely some sort of scary, manly place. And he was taking me there.

"If it's gross and dirty, I'm not going to be happy."

"It is neither gross nor dirty."

"Cool. Then I promise not to tell anyone about it."

"Just like that?"

"Yup." And yeah, like a teenager, I popped my P. Had to make a point. "What you do is your business. Besides, the *last* person I'd tell is Alder."

"You can't tell Elijah either."

"That's fine. He's keeping secrets from me, so this is turnabout."

"What sorts of secrets?"

"Well, I mean, it's obvious he's doing something with—" I bit my lip, wanting so badly to pull the words back. To have shut up before I'd ever mentioned that. "Shit."

"You're talking about him and Zane. Like...dating?"

"You know?"

He shrugged. "I'm guessing, but they seem awfully chummy."

"I wish I hadn't opened my mouth." I sat a little deeper, biting my lip. "I mean...it's not my secret, you know? And no one here—"

"Hey." Deacon reached over, laying his hand on my thigh. "I'm not asking you to out your brother. I've been a bartender a long time and stared through sniper scopes for days on end before that. I'm good at judging people, is all."

"You won't tell Alder or Bishop?"

He glanced my way, shooting me a wink. "You keep my secret, I'll keep yours."

"Technically Elijah's."

"True. All secrets can be held in the vault. It's no one's business, anyway."

"Like our night together—no one's business."

He squeezed my thigh a little tighter. "It's just between us. For now."

Butterflies exploded in my stomach. *For now* meant...well, I assumed it meant we'd tell people eventually. Which meant either he was going to burn his friendship with my brother to the ground by telling him he'd fucked and run on me—something I highly doubted —or there would be...

More.

I really liked the idea of more.

I held that happy little thought in my mind as Deacon drove out of town and up into the mountains. There were a bunch of little cabins out that way—hunting properties and vacation homes, mostly. Not too many people actually lived this far out. Deacon eventually turned onto a rocky road that should have really been named a path, cutting through towering pine trees. The road followed a steep incline with one side solid rock jutting straight up and the other...well, it seemed pretty treacherous on his side. I kept my mouth shut and let him drive, hoping like hell he'd done this enough times to be able to get us up the hill and back down. He certainly seemed calm. And apparently, I did not.

"Don't worry," he said out of the blue. "It looks a lot more dangerous than it is."

"Really?"

"No, but I don't want you to break your hand holding the oh-shit handle, and it sounded good."

I let go of the overhead handle and sat back, taking a couple deep breaths to soothe my nerves.

"There we go," Deacon finally said as he made a turn at the top of the hill. A small wooden cabin sat in the middle of a clearing. A normal clearing without deadly drop-offs and craggy rock walls. The entire area looked quaint and tidy, not at all decrepit or scary. In fact, the cabin almost looked like some sort of magical residence, like the home of a green witch with lots of herbs growing inside. Or maybe...

"Is this your fairy cabin?"

Deacon chuckled and shook his head. "I told you...we do not invite the fae into our homes."

"So, no Shye. Got it."

He laughed and hopped down from the truck, hurrying over to hold my door and offer me a hand.

"Be careful," he said as soon as I stepped foot on the hard ground. "It's rocky out here."

"Such a gentleman."

He grinned. "Nah, I just like watching your boobs bounce when you get up and down from my truck."

I smacked his arm. Not that I was really mad. I liked flirty Deacon. A lot. Too much.

"So," I said, trying hard to stay on target. "What are we doing here?"

His smile fell, and his expression grew serious. "We're arming ourselves."

I looked at the house then back at him, letting my thoughts wander. Putting pieces together—former Special Services soldier, barkeep, Alder's right-hand man. "You supply the team with weapons."

He stood stock-still, staring at me, before finally nodding once.

I shrugged. "Cool."

"That's it? Cool?"

"Were you expecting me to judge you for your procurement skills?" I frowned and started walking for the cabin. "I may not be Alder's biggest fan, but I'm still a Kennard, and logistics are a necessity in any sort of business. Come on, old man. Let's go see what toys you have in there."

DEACON

The woman was the biggest threat I'd ever come across. Sexy, beautiful, smart, observant...and flirting with me. There was no way this day was going to end the way it needed to.

I opened the door to the cabin and stood back, letting Lainie walk in first. Watching her. My gut felt leaden, and my heart thumped hard in my chest. This place—this little cabin in the woods —was my respite. My secret hideaway. Sure, I hid a lot of weapons in it, but that wasn't the main purpose of the place. This was my secret getaway, and someone else was there.

Someone was judging my soul.

"It's so lovely," she said, her voice soft and sounding almost in awe.

I looked around, trying to see the room through her eyes. I'd removed the ceiling to showcase the support beams that had once been hidden in a useless attic space. The floors were a deep, dark brown wood meeting up to soft gray walls that looked almost white in the lighting. There was no traditional floor plan to the space—no living room with a couch and chair or television. There was a small kitchen in the back, a large rug before it, one stack of foam rectangles called a Nugget, oddly enough, and mounds upon mounds of pillows stacked into a pile.

Definitely not the normal living room setup.

"Like I said," I murmured, my voice tight. "I don't ever let people in here."

She looked over her shoulder at me, her smile so soft and sweet. "Thank you for allowing me to see this. It's perfect."

"Yeah?"

"Yeah. I love all the pillows."

"You don't think it's weird that I don't have furniture?"

"You don't need it. You can make any sort of comfy seating arrangement with the pillows." She shot me a wink over her shoulder. "Or lying."

She was so fucking perfect. "That's...yeah. That's what I do."

Lainie slipped off her shoes and stepped deeper into the cabin, running her fingers along whatever surface she came across.

"The entire space is just so warm and rich and...soft." Another look over her shoulder, a smile that held the sort of promises any man would sell his soul to accept. "It's like a little love shack."

I laughed, unable not to. "Yeah, a self-love shack. I never bring anyone here, remember?"

She lifted her chin toward the stack of pillows, her expression seeking permission. I nodded once but didn't join her, didn't move closer as she made herself comfortable. I couldn't. This image—a gorgeous woman accepting and enjoying the simplicity of my cabin —was a dream come true. One too impossible to have even contemplated. I'd never dreamed of such a thing because it had seemed impossible, yet there we were.

I had no idea what to do with myself.

"This is lovely," she said, stretching onto some of the larger pillows. "Who needs furniture?"

"Fuck," I hissed, my cock hard as stone and my entire body needy and ready and wanting. "I need to..."

There was no finishing that statement. I rushed through the big room and toward what was supposed to be a bedroom. I didn't use it as such, though. There was no bed, no dresser or nightstand. There were only gun cabinets and weaponry lockers. It took me two keys to enter the room and a passcode typed into an electric keypad. I'd even covered the windows so no one could access the space. This was a gold mine I didn't want anyone else to get their hands on.

I probably should have shut the door behind me, but something about having Lainie there, about her energy in my space, made me almost want her to see this. To know. To understand this side of me.

"Whoa." As I'd both hoped for and sort of dreaded, Lainie slipped in behind me, looking around with wide eyes. "This is all…"

Honesty time.

"Guns. Bombs. Various defensive and offensive weaponry." I pointed toward a locker. "There are poisons and listening devices in there, knives and swords and other silent killers on the one above it, and a few rocket launchers in the closet."

"No night vision equipment?"

I indicated the door behind her with a lift of my chin. "That's in the linen closet outside the bathroom."

Her face went slack. Her expression one I couldn't read. "I was only kidding."

Oh. "Well… Okay."

I opened a trunk and started the process of inventorying, stocking, arming, and prepping to bring the equipment with me. Everyone on my team needed to be well armed with weapons they could be comfortable with. I'd worked with Zane—that man could handle anything. Elijah looked like a guy who liked a rifle, but I planned on bringing him a few handguns as well. Lainie…

Fuck. Lainie was likely going to end up in the line of fire with me.

That thought burned a hole in my soul I wasn't prepared for.

"Here," I said, my voice too gruff and demanding. My fear not allowing me to soften it. "Hold this."

She took the gun from my hand, staring down at it. "What is it?"

"It's a Sig Sauer P238. It's got an easy racking slide and is petite enough for you to conceal. It doesn't have a lot of kickback either."

"You realize I'm from Justice."

I froze, staring up at her, her words not making sense. "Yeah?"

She handed me the Sig Sauer back. "I've been shooting since I was a toddler. I can handle something more than this."

The woman was a siren, singing songs specifically to attract me. To entice me into her embrace and seduce me. I'd likely end up broken and lifeless on the rocks of her shores, but it didn't matter. The song was worth it.

"You realize that may have been the sexiest thing you could have ever said to me, right?"

She rolled those blue eyes I loved so much. "Quit being such a guy and tell me what you're arming me with."

Fuck me. That was it, the tug that broke my chain. The one that tightened the leash. We had no time—had enemies right on our tail—but I couldn't resist another second. I jumped to my feet and grabbed her, laying a kiss on her lips that I'd needed like no other. Gripping her thighs and pulling until she hopped and wrapped her legs around my waist. I carried my woman back to the pillows and dropped down with her on me, needing her heat and her flesh and her whimpers. Wanting to lose myself in her even if it destroyed my life in Justice.

"Deacon," she gasped when we broke for the kiss enough for me to slide my tongue down her neck. "We don't have a lot of time."

"Minutes. I know." I bit down, growling when she arched and

gasped. When her fingers dug into my shoulders. "I need to make you come, beautiful. So bad."

She pushed at my shoulders, making me freeze. But her shove wasn't to stop me; it was to flip me over so she could roll on top of me. She straddled my hips and yanked that whole, long dress over her head, revealing herself to me in one move. Practically naked underneath all that billowy fabric.

"So fucking gorgeous." I jackknifed up and slid my arms behind her, unhooking her bra. Tossing it to the side. Sliding my hands over her chest and grabbing her breasts to knead and massage. To watch her head fall back and her mouth open as I assaulted her the way I knew she liked. Naked. I had my Lainie—my *Elaine*—naked on my lap again. And I wasn't going to squander this opportunity. "I would give up my entire life to make you mine."

She rolled her head forward, those blue eyes meeting mine. Curling her body over mine to lay a kiss on my lips. To taste and bite and breathe into me. To rock her hips over mine and tease the fuck out of my cock.

"Minutes," she finally said, one hand holding me by the neck and the other slipping between us to tug on the fly of my jeans. "We only have a few minutes."

"I can make you come three times in those minutes."

She bit my lip hard enough to make me jump before rolling back and giving me a smile filled with a siren's confidence. And her malfeasance.

"Prove it."

Chapter Sixteen

LAINIE

I had no idea what it was about Deacon in his natural habitat that turned me on so much. The dichotomy of the space and the way he fit into both so seamlessly intrigued, though. From the pillows, the softness, the obvious almost childlike desire to furnish a space so out of the norm, to the armory in the bedroom. He was a puzzle that I had a feeling the solution to lay right there in that little cabin in the woods. I just had to look for it.

The first place I was going to look was in that mound of pillows. Once I got the man naked.

"Lainie," he said, the groan underlying his words something that made me feel even more powerful over him.

"No." I pushed him back and tugged his pants down his legs, shuffling on my knees to strip him. "Not here. Not in this space. I don't want to be Lainie here."

Deacon stared up at me, his usually bright green eyes dark with desire. His hands reaching for me even before I got the words out. He knew what I wanted. Knew what we needed to go back to. He knew what I needed, and the man was nothing if not a giver.

"Get up here, Elaine."

Fuck me, the shiver that demand—that *word*—sent down my spine went straight to my clit. I could have come right there from hearing him call me Elaine again. Wanted to. I followed his guidance, crawling over him until he had me where he wanted me.

Which was sitting right over his face.

"Deacon, we don't have time—"

I sweated and grabbed his hair at the first lick, the shot of pleasure cutting off all abilities to put words together and make sense.

Deacon chuckled against me, teasing me with soft licks and kisses. "If it's between railing you across the floor or eating this pussy, I'll eat this pussy."

"Such a charmer." I leaned back, giving in to my body's desire to let him do what he wanted to. Pleasure spiking and roiling through me like a storm as he sucked and teased my clit. When he added a few fingers into the mix, slipping them inside me and making me want to scream, I stretched to grab his hard cock and give it a few strokes.

I may not have been able to get my mouth on him in this position, but two could play at this game.

"Fuck, beautiful," he said from underneath me, still so close I could feel his lips move against my wet flesh. Still filling me with his fingers. "I want to be inside you."

I tried to pull away, to move down his body, but he held me in place. Once again sucking my clit between his lips and making me squeal.

"If you want to be inside me," I finally said, my words way too breathy to be normal. "You have to stop what you're doing."

"Come first, fuck second."

I did so love a man with a plan.

Deacon focused his energies on bringing me up and over that hill of pleasure, on doing everything he already knew I liked and adding a few more tricks to his repertoire as if testing their ability to get me off. The man was a champ at licking pussy, and it only took a few minutes for me to be gyrating on his face as I held on. As I rocked over him and truly rode his mouth. As I came all over him with a groan that would embarrass me when I thought about it later.

He didn't wait for a single moment after he made me come. He gave me no time to recover or catch my breath. One second, I was astride his face, trembling and mumbling nonsense. The next, I was sitting on his hips as he impaled me with his cock. Filled me with it. As he slid inside where he'd made me so wet and sloppy.

"Fuck, you're so tight." He arched his back and tugged down on my hips, thrusting deeper. Making me cry out. "Condom?"

"Birth control."

"Fucking smart woman. Tell me if it hurts."

"It does. It hurts." I placed a hand on his hip when he froze, gripping him. Trying to pull him deeper. "I like the sting of you filling me."

"So fucking naughty." He began to move again, pumping himself in and out from underneath me. That wouldn't do, though. I was on top for a reason, and I wanted the control.

So, I took it.

Placing both hands on Deacon's chest, I stared down at him and rolled my hips. Taking him deeper. Pulling him almost all the way out on the same move before swallowing him back up. He squeezed his eyes closed and bit his lip, gripping my hips tighter. Changing his moves to match mine. Once I had him mirroring me, once I had the basic idea of what was coming, I let go. I took full control and rode him at a pace that suited my needs.

I fucked him like he deserved to be fucked.

"Elaine. I need—" He arched and moaned as I rocked over him, lifting up and down on his cock. Pinching his nipples and angling my hips so he could fill me as deeply as possible. "Fuck, I need you to come. You have to come, beautiful."

"If I don't?"

He chuckled, the sound strained. "I'm going to lose my mind trying to hold off."

I reached behind me and grabbed his balls, massaging them. Loving the way his body tensed and he gasped at the contact.

"I want to see it," I said, still riding him. Still pushing him. "I love watching you break."

Deacon grunted but took control from me, shifting his arms to grab me and lift me up in the same rhythm. To use me like some sort of sex doll to jack off his cock. He bit my neck then leaned down to take my nipple into his mouth, one hand slipping between us to put pressure on my clit. That thumb was the devil in my bid to outlast him, a cheating bastard in the competition to who would orgasm first.

He was going to win.

"I wanted to make you come," I whined, dropping my head onto his shoulder as the pleasure began to tingle throughout my body. "I wanted to be in control."

"Oh, Elaine. You *are* in control." He rolled us to the side, pulling my leg high up his arm and holding it in the crook of his elbow. Opening me wide so he could fuck me and press that evil thumb against my clit. "You've been in control since the moment we met. I could have you underneath me and be fucking you across this floor, could have you tied up and laid out naked for me, and you'd still be in control."

I planted a kiss on him as the pleasure broke, as my body locked into place for that brief, two-second interval between actively seeking an orgasm and receiving one. That moment of pure bliss and anticipation colliding into one, soul-breaking moment. The feel of his lips on mine, the taste of him, shattered what little control of my body I had. As my orgasm rolled through me, I jerked and shook and trembled all over Deacon. Falling apart. Knowing he'd be there to put the pieces back together.

He grunted and thrust into me, chanting my name—my full name—as he came inside me. As our bodies pushed each other over the edge and crashed together into the sloppy, messy dance of climaxing. As he said my name one last time and grabbed my hips with a grip that I knew would leave bruises.

I couldn't wait to see them.

I couldn't wait to get more of them.

Couldn't wait to show them off to him.

A badge of honor. A sign of ownership. Whatever—he was going to like them. I already knew that.

Chapter Seventeen

DEACON

I ran a finger over the blue marks along Lainie's hip, chuckling when she smacked my hand away.

"I'm trying to get dressed."

Sadly, that was true. She was *trying* to get dressed. Something I'd already done. Not because either of us wanted to don clothes and leave the little cabin in the woods, but because we had to. There was a motorcycle gang wanting to talk to me, and we needed to get that accomplished. Today. Now. Basically, only minutes after I'd had that woman naked and riding me.

My timing was stellar.

"I bruised you." I caught her eye and grinned. "I'd say I'm sorry, but I'm totally not."

She rose onto the balls of her feet and kissed me right there in the living room. All soft lips and that sweet taste I couldn't get enough of.

"I don't want you to be sorry," she said as she dropped the skirt of her flowy dress, hiding her soft skin from me once again. "I'm certainly not. I actually can't wait to see more of them on me."

And that, friends, was why I was going to fall so far in love with this woman that I'd never crawl back up from under her.

But first...reality.

Once dressed and ready to go, I stocked the truck with the weaponry and defensive armature I thought we might need. I even brought along an extra gun for Lainie—one with a little more heft and firepower. The woman could hold her own, and she deserved a weapon that matched her power.

Me? I was a schoolboy with one hell of a crush.

"Gimme."

Lainie glanced my way, glancing down at my hand—the one I held open and stretched out toward her—with a confused look. "Give you what?"

"Your hand. I want it."

She placed her hand in mine, and I lifted it to my mouth, kissing the back before weaving our fingers together. I rested our joined show of affection on my thigh.

"That's better."

"What's gotten into you?"

"You have."

She didn't reply, but I saw that smile grow. She even bit her lip as if trying to hold back the grin. After a moment of joyous silence, she unbuckled her seat belt and scooched across the bench, coming to sit in the middle seat. To put her body right next to mine.

"Buckle back up," I said, giving her back her hand so she could secure herself, then grabbing it again. Another kiss, another moment of our digits interlacing, and then we were quiet once more. Her beside me. Holding hands.

Two decades ago—when I was young and still in high school—this would have been my idea of heaven. Now, I was older, had been through some shit, and knew better. Back in the cabin, in that moment after we'd come together, when we were lying on the pillows in the silence with our sweaty bodies tangled together...that had been an updated version of my heaven. One I was desperate to get back to.

Instead, I drove us to the Jury Room. My stomach actually sank as we pulled into the parking lot. Our little moment was over...for now.

"Looks like Zane and Elijah are already here," I said. I gave her hand one last kiss then shifted on my seat so I could look her square in the eye. "You ready for this?"

She shrugged one shoulder, staring toward the door to the building. "I can handle my brother and Zane."

"Are you sure you want to be involved at all? I can take you home, Lainie. Can get you away—"

"No." Her tone, the harshness of her word, shut me right down. "I'm in on this. Don't try to hide me away like some weak little girl who can't protect herself."

"I don't see you as weak or as a little girl. I see you as someone precious to me. If you're worried, I'll help you get to some place safe where you can hole up until this is over."

"The only thing I'm worried about is you."

That honesty, that vulnerability, gutted me. I grabbed her neck and tugged her close, kissing her deeply. Needing one last connection like I needed air to breathe.

"I want this all over with," I whispered when we broke apart, keeping her forehead against mine.

"What are you going to do when it is?"

"Go on a vacation. With you. To an island with a lot of fucking beaches."

"That sounds perfect."

"Christmas in the islands?"

She clung to my shirt, tugging me closer. "Will this be over by Christmas?"

I didn't have an answer for her, but I hoped. I really hoped.

"We should get inside," I said, and I couldn't help but notice the way her shoulders fell. The small sigh she let out. My not answering was noticed and not appreciated. But I didn't want to promise her something I couldn't come through on. I didn't want to make plans when I had no idea how the next twenty-four hours would go.

But I had plans forming. Good ones. And I was a determined motherfucker.

"Don't forget your gun," I said before leading her out of the truck and heading for the bar.

"Hey," Elijah hollered when I finally opened the door for Lainie. "We were about to call out a search party for you two."

"Hardy har har. You can't just throw a couple guns in a truck and drive off, kid. There's ammunition to worry about and stuff like bulletproof vests to bring along. That shit takes time to load up."

He grinned as if he totally didn't believe me. "That's a fine story to tell Alder about why you two were gone for so long."

I was about to answer him when the door opened. I spun, grabbing Lainie and shoving her behind me. Turning to face...

"Camden?" I let go of Lainie, taking a step toward the man. "What are you doing here?"

Cam turned those dead eyes my way, looking like a shark who

wasn't yet hungry but could still rip you apart at any moment. Just for fun. "I thought I could be of service."

No, he didn't. He thought Coyote was mixed in with the crew in town. Camden wasn't here to be a teammate; he was here to settle a score. Whether that played for or against the rest of us remained to be seen.

"Hey, Cam." Lainie slipped past me, wrapping her arms around Camden and pulling him in for a hug. Something dark and fiery lit in my belly, the spark of an emotion I hated. One that left me glaring after Camden, not liking the possessive way he stood next to Lainie. Hating the casual way they spoke to each other. The flirty way.

"What's happening, Penny Lane?" Camden left his arm around her shoulders and walked the two of them toward the bar. "Let's have a beer and get some planning done. I'm ready to bitch-slap some bikers."

This was not going to go as I'd thought it was.

LAINIE

Deacon was throwing a bit of a tantrum.

"You okay there, Deac?" Elijah said after the fourth time the man had slammed a bottle down on the bar top.

"Fine. I can't find anything I need, though." He tore through the couple of cupboards behind the big, wooden structure where the rest of the group sat. Looking more and more irritated as he closed cabinets without retrieving whatever it was he wanted.

"Can I help you find something?"

"No." His green eyes met mine, sliding to the side where Camden sat right up against me before looking away. "It's probably in the back."

With that, he stormed out of the room. I was just thinking I should follow him when Camden leaned in to whisper to me.

"He does know we've been friends since like birth, right?"

I shifted so I could put a little space between us then threw a weak punch at his shoulder. "Behave."

He moved away, smiling as he brought his beer bottle to his mouth. "Just asking because he sure is giving me dirty looks right now."

I couldn't argue with that. Deacon had been grumpy since Camden had walked through the door. Whether he had a problem with Camden himself or Camden with *me*, I had no idea. I was going to ask, though. Once he calmed down a little.

"Come on, Zane," Elijah said as he slid off his barstool. "Let's sort through all the weaponry Deacon brought and start laying out the supplies."

Zane—looking more and more like a really handsome and built Buddy Holly the longer I spent with him—threw back the last of his beer and nodded. "Sounds like a plan."

Which left me alone with Camden. That was an opportunity I hadn't been expecting but was definitely going to take advantage of.

"I'm sorry," I started, knowing this was likely not the thought path he'd want to go down. "I'm real sorry about Leah and that I couldn't be here for her funeral."

Camden's energy changed, his body going stiff and his eyes locking on a blank spot across from us. "It's fine. Finn told me you had some sort of test thing."

My master's thesis presentation, but I wasn't going to correct him. "It's not fine—I should have been here. She was my friend..."

I sniffed, trying hard not to let the unshed tears fall. The loss of Leah—the murder that took her from us—was still too new. Too fresh. The pain hadn't been tucked away just yet for me, which meant it had to be a million times worse for Cam.

"Remember that summer when the seven of us—you, Mercy, Finn, Elijah, Leah, Anabeth, and me—went camping?"

I nodded, hazy pictures of summer nights with all of us drinking and dancing and having fun in the woods—long before most of us were anywhere near legal to do so—flitting through my mind.

"You and Leah kept disappearing."

"We kept running off to have sex," Cam said, almost smiling. "We thought we were being slick."

"We knew."

He sighed, a small lift of his lips dancing across his face for just the briefest of moments. "Those were good days."

I picked at the label on the beer bottle in my hand, the weight of grief and loss heavy on my shoulders. "They really were."

I took another deep breath, knowing the conversation needed to shift. That we had too much to do to get bogged down in the sort of pain remembering Leah would bring.

"So, tell me, Camden Reese—"

"Oh fuck," he said before he downed the last of his beer. "You only use my full name when you're about to say something I won't like."

"That's not true."

"Over two decades of hanging out with you would prove otherwise."

I rolled my eyes. "Fine. Camden—just Camden—where the hell have you been all these months?"

"Been chasing Leah's killer." His smile fell, his face hardening. He took a quick sip of his beer. "I was in California when Finn texted me that the fucker was in town. I hauled ass back."

That tone, that voice—it wasn't the Camden I knew so well. It wasn't the fun-loving kid who'd kissed Leah every chance he got. It wasn't the man who'd helped me pack my car to move to Denver while he was on leave from the Marines. The Camden I knew had always had a bit of a temper, but the low simmering rage I felt in his words was new. And heartbreaking.

"I mean... What are you going to do about that, though?"

The world shrank. There was nothing but Camden and me, just the two of us existing. There was no bar, no town, no structure. We were alone in the universe in a moment that hung so very heavy upon my shoulders. I knew his answer before he said it, knew where his mind went when he thought about Leah's killer. I knew what losing Leah had done to him, and right then, I felt it too.

He looked me square in the eye, his completely dead. Flat. Sharklike. "I'm going to kill him."

"That's murder." The words were out before I could stop them, the weapon thrown before I could restrain myself.

Camden simply shrugged off the accusation. "He nailed the window shut, locked the door from the outside, waited for Leah to fall asleep, and set our fucking house on fire. Bishop can tell me all he wants that Leah looked as if she'd never woken up, but I know better. That woman couldn't sleep through anything—I used to joke that she could hear a mouse pissing on a cotton ball. She woke up. She suffered. She was afraid." He paused, took a big gulp of his beer, and let out a breath. "This Coyote guy needs to be afraid too."

I had a moment, just a small one, where something inside my head agreed with Cam. Where his goal seemed less illegal and more deserved. Just a tiny spot of time, though, because a crash sounded from the kitchen and stole all the attention. The room spun back into focus, the noises and scents returning. I unintentionally put a foot down on the floor and slid my weight that way, ready to run to the back and check on Deacon. Needing to see him, grab him, feel his arms around me. To connect.

Camden must have noticed the way I was almost frozen—half on and half off the barstool. He saw, and he obviously understood my hesitation. "Go on, Lainie. I'm fine. Go take care of your man."

"He's not mine," I said, the words almost automatic. The sound so very wrong.

Camden must have felt the same way because he chuckled all low and dark. "Of course he is. You just have to be willing to take him."

That statement didn't make sense to me, but it didn't matter. Another crash sounded, and I was on my feet and moving before he finished speaking. I found Deacon in the very back of the kitchen, washing large metal sheet pans with an aggression that made me pause.

But I wasn't afraid of Deacon Manns. Never had been. "Deacon."

He froze for a second but didn't turn around. Instead, he went right back to scrubbing the pan in his hands. Ignoring me. My heart broke a little for him, my need to be close to him making me choke on a sob. I must have made a sound, because he turned again, green eyes finding mine. Something he saw on my face must have worried him, because he was in motion immediately. I took a single step forward and then was right where I wanted to be—in his arms. Completely wrapped up in his feel and his scent and the sound of his breathing.

The world righted itself just enough for me to find purchase once more.

"Deacon." I trembled, shaking in his arms as he picked me up off the floor and carried me into a back room that looked like an office.

"What did he do to you?"

I shook my head, because this wasn't about Camden. This wasn't about the fear I felt for him or the way his energy sucked the universe into his black hole of anger and depression. This was about Deacon and me and how much I needed him in that moment. So instead of speaking, I kissed him. Not lightly, not soft. No. I kissed him deep and long, putting all my passion into that act. Gripping his shoulders and holding him against me so I could absorb some of his warmth. I kissed him like I would die without the taste of him.

And in that moment, I just might have.

Still, I had to make fun of him. Just a little. So, I kept my arms around him when we broke the kiss, and I gave him a sweet peck on the nose before saying, "I like you jealous."

"I'm not jealous."

I raised my eyebrows, watching him. Waiting him out.

"Okay, fine. I'm jealous of the way you and Camden seemed all flirty," he said with a sigh. Then he grabbed my ass and tugged me closer, dipping his head to nuzzle into my neck. Biting me a little. "Can you blame me, beautiful?"

"Cam and I have been friends practically since birth. There's nothing to be jealous about."

Deacon grunted but didn't argue with me. One more kiss, one last moment of sweetness, and I rose to my feet and untangled myself from his hold.

"Come on," I said, reaching for him. Needing his hand in mine to keep me in the moment. "Quit pouting back here, and let's go plan some murders."

He followed willingly enough but stopped before we reached the door and yanked me against him again. Clutching me to him, my back to his front. Running one hand over my hip—over the bruises he'd left there—and the other up to clutch at my breast over my clothes.

"Deac—"

"You could be walking out there as Mrs. Elaine Manns instead of Lainie Kennard, and I'd still be jealous. How could I not be?"

I shook my head, gripping his hand. Hanging on. "I've never done anything to make someone jealous."

He spun me around, dropping another kiss to my lips before whispering, "Any man who had you on his arm and wasn't jealous of others even getting to see your gorgeous smile was an idiot. You're worth being jealous over."

The man made my insides go liquid, made me blush and get butterflies in my stomach like when I was a child and had a crush. But I was no child, and this wasn't just a crush. I knew it. He knew it. What we were going to do about it... Well. We'd come to that.

I grabbed his hand again and dragged him toward the door, looking over my shoulder as I said, "Who said I would change my last name when we got married anyway?"

"When, huh?"

"When what?"

His grin widened, an arrogant sort of *I win* look on his handsome face. "You said *when* we got married."

I rolled back the tape in my head, trying hard not to show how unsurprised I was. *Casual. Keep it casual.*

"I meant if."

He tugged me to a stop right by the door and leaned over me. Brushing his nose against mine as he whispered, "No, you didn't."

And with that, he walked out into the bar, holding the door for me and waiting all expectantly for me to walk through it. To follow him.

Which, of course, I did.

Because he was right. I hadn't meant if.

I'd said when.

I was picking my future with a single word, and that future included him and me together.

We just had to figure out how to make that happen.

Chapter Eighteen

DEACON

Something wouldn't let my brain rest.

I sat at the bar with Elijah, Zane, and Camden. All three of them plotting and planning how to track down the Soul Suckers. How to find them. Lainie worked the room, listening and attentive but unable to sit still. I understood that sensation because I felt the same but didn't know why. I was missing something.

Lainie caught me looking at her and smiled, immediately coming around to place a hand on my shoulder. To surround me with her scent.

Fuck me, but I was falling in love with this woman.

I grabbed her hand and kissed her palm, wishing I could figure out what I wasn't seeing so I could settle down. She dropped a kiss near my ear.

"You okay?" she whispered, as if sensing the agitation within me.

I wasn't really sure how to answer that question, but I tried to give her something. Kept my voice low so our conversation stayed between just the two of us. "I think so."

"You sure? Because you look like you're ready to run through the walls to get out of here."

"Why would I run if you're here?"

She chuckled. "Wouldn't matter if you did anyway. I know how to find you."

And that was the moment the penny dropped. She knew how to find me. Everyone knew how to find me.

Why were we working so hard?

"Fuck," I hissed, loud enough to snag the attention of the other guys in the room.

"What?" Elijah asked, frowning.

"We don't need to look for them—they're planning to find us." I was up and moving before I made the conscious decision to, hurrying to the stash of weapons Zane and Elijah had stacked on the opposite side of the room. "We've been everywhere looking for them, seeing glimpses but not finding them. Always a few steps behind. That was intentional. When they wanted to make contact—the night they caught Lainie and me in my truck—they found me. We think we've been hunting them, but they've been playing hide-and-seek."

Zane didn't sound convinced. "You think they'll just...show up?"

"They did it that night at my truck. They'll do it again."

"So, what do we do?"

I nodded toward Lainie. "Elijah needs to take her home."

"No," Elijah said, arguing as I knew he'd do. "I'm not leaving."

"Yes, you are. Zane and Camden can hang with me, but I want Lainie out of here."

Lainie's face—so gorgeous and expressive—hardened. Her eyes going dark as she glared at me. "I thought you weren't a sexist prick?"

I hurried across the floor, grabbing her. Tugging her into my arms without a care for who saw. Kissing her right there in front of her brother and our friends because I had to. Thankfully, she didn't resist me, but she certainly didn't melt into me the way I would have liked. I'd pissed her off, and I needed to make her understand why.

"Beautiful," I murmured when we broke apart. "You are my biggest weakness. If they even look at you cross-eyed, I will lose my shit. I need to focus, and for that, I need you to be home and safe with someone watching over you."

"I'm not weak."

"No, but I am. When it comes to you." Another kiss. Relishing in the feel of her softening against me. "They're going to come for me. They *want* to talk to me for some reason, and they know exactly how to find me. If you're with me when they show, I'll..."

I couldn't even finish my sentence, couldn't fathom the level of instinctual rage I would feel if they even looked her way. Camden had lost his wife, plus Alder and I had seen firsthand the depravity these fuckers played in when we'd gone to kill Shye's stepbrother and ended up rescuing Jinx. No way could I handle my Lainie getting caught up in that world.

But she was mad and hurt, her body stiff and her voice silent. I was screwing everything up.

"Please, baby," I whispered, pleading in the only way I knew how. "I know you can hold your own. I know you can fight and shoot. I want you secured, though. I just—" I shook my head, meeting her eyes dead on and laying my truth right there at her feet. "I just pulled my head out of my ass and figured out you're the only woman I will ever want. I can't lose you already. I would murder every fucking one of them for even breathing in your direction."

Lainie's expression softened, and she ran a finger down my face, still looking upset but not nearly as angry as before. Inching closer as she said, "Fine. I'll leave. But I'm going to yell at you about this later."

"And I'll sit through it because I know I deserve it." I had never felt more relief than in that moment. I chuckled and kissed her again, quicker this time. "Don't forget your gun."

"Like I need a handgun in the apartment. Let's not get crazy." She sighed and pulled away, looking to her brother. "Take me home, Jeeves."

Elijah looked about as unhappy as she was. "We don't even get to pull straws for who takes guard duty?"

Zane answered that one. "Nope. You're up, champ. Take care of your sister. That's more important than hanging here and waiting for the possibility of Deacon being wrong."

The two shared a look, one I could feel from across the room. One filled with emotion—maybe anguish, maybe anger. I was too far away to tell. But then Elijah huffed and spun, leading Lainie out the door without another word. The two of them disappearing into the night.

I gave Zane a solid twenty seconds before I asked, "Better?"

He turned those dark eyes on me, his expression blank. "Don't know what you mean."

"Sure, you do. You and Elijah." I shot a look to Camden, who seemed just as interested in this whole scene as I did. "You see it too, right, Cam?"

The former Marine nodded. "Absolutely. Elijah's cool as fuck, too. Good choice."

Zane sighed and looked up toward the ceiling, still tense. "How did you figure it out?"

That was an easy one. "Because you look at him the way I feel like I look at his sister."

He pinned me with a glare, a challenging one. "You planning on telling her brothers that?"

He'd said brothers, but I knew he meant Alder. The oldest, the most protective, and the one with the worst temper. The one who'd been my best friend and had saved my life a few times over the course of the last couple decades. Was I planning on telling him that I was in love with his little sister?

"You bet your fucking ass I am."

Camden huffed something that was close to a laugh from where he still sat at the bar, shaking his head in the process. "You two are in for a wild ride, being with Kennards."

I shrugged, and Zane did the same. Camden wasn't wrong, but it didn't matter. I was all in on Lainie. And once I got rid of these fucking bikers, I was going to tell her. And Alder.

I was still standing in place, my head swirling with that knowledge, when my phone rang. I reached for it on instinct, my brow pulling tight when I saw the name on the screen.

"It's Lainie," I said. Camden and Zane both turned my way, looking just as confused as I felt. Why would she be calling so soon?

I tapped the screen to answer the call. "You okay, beautiful?"

The voice that came through the line wasn't Lainie, though. It wasn't even female.

"She's fine...for the moment. We've been waiting for a chance to talk to you, barkeep."

I darted a look almost instinctually to the handgun on the bar. The one I'd selected for Lainie. The one she'd left behind. She was on the road with only her brother, unarmed, and obviously, someone had gotten to her. My mind switched from normal, everyday Deacon to military sniper in an instant. No, beyond that. Because what I'd said to Lainie earlier had been true—I would kill any motherfucker who even breathed in her direction.

I don't know if they came to Justice looking for an outright war, but they were about to get one.

"You've fucked up, son," I replied, my voice hard as nails and my mind already swirling with how I was going to slaughter the bastard on the other end of the line. "You have fucked up big-time."

Chapter Nineteen

LAINIE

I can't believe I have to babysit you."

"I can't believe they think I need to be babysat." I sat deeper in the front seat of Elijah's car, arms crossed and mood sour. "This has been the longest week ever."

"Tell me about it." Elijah gunned the engine, speeding his way down the highway toward Main Street. "I can't believe they kicked us out right as the good stuff was coming together. Did they think you can't hold your own? Am I the weakest link?"

"They're going to need more help than they think."

"Yeah." He gripped the steering wheel tighter, frowning. "They don't realize it yet, but I think you're right."

"It's like they think we need protecting."

"Right?" He took a curve smoothly, the car purring down the road. Going way too fast for the speed limit, but it wasn't like there were local police to worry about. "I would have kept you safe. I'm attentive and can handle a gun just fine. It's like Deacon doesn't trust—"

"Eli!"

A flash of something dark out of the corner of my eye, a reach for my brother's arm, and then there was nothing but chaos. Noises as if from a horror movie and the world spinning. Or maybe we were spinning. Elijah yelled something just before everything went upside down. Something hit my head, or my head hit something—I couldn't tell. Couldn't figure out where we were or what was happening. All I knew was noise and movement and the sickening feeling that something had just gone very, very wrong.

And pain.

———

The first thing that registered once my brain decided to come back online was that my head hurt. Shoulder, too. The second thing was that my shoulder was hurting because I was hanging upside down and the seat belt was biting into it as it supported my weight.

Upside

Down

"E," I said, the sound thick and slow, my mouth and tongue not quite working together the way I wanted them to. "Eli. You okay?"

Nothing. I got nothing back. I tried to turn my head, but there wasn't a lot of room, plus my eyes didn't seem to be able to focus. Everything appeared a little blurry, a little overlapped and double vision-like. Once, while hiking with Anabeth and Finn, I'd taken a nasty stumble and landed with my head on a rock. The hit had been hard, the headache and nausea immediate. I'd been able to walk out with the help of the others, but that dizzy, disassociated feeling in my brain had stuck around for weeks. A concussion, the doctors had said. I had no idea what I'd hit my head on this time, but it was obvious to me that I had done some damage. Maybe another concussion, maybe something worse. I couldn't tell yet.

Needing to get my body to do what I asked it to, I closed my eyes and took some deep breaths. Following the pattern of the metronome in my head. It took a number of seconds for me to realize that the rhythmic clicking wasn't a metronome—it was the sound of something dripping at a steady interval.

My eyes popped open, and I instinctually looked down. Or up... but down. My head hurt too much to make the distinction. There was blood on the roof of the car. Both under me and where Elijah would be. Should be. His seat was empty.

"Eli!" This time, my voice worked a little better, though yelling caused something much worse than simple pain to stab me in the eye and make me gag. "Elijah! Where...oh."

I wanted to clutch my head so badly, but moving my arms seemed difficult and my brain was not about to cooperate. I closed my eyes to recenter myself again and took a few deep breaths.

"You're awake."

The male voice—one I didn't recognize—made me jerk and scream, both things my poor brain didn't like. I tried looking to my right to see who was there, but I couldn't turn enough. I had a feeling it didn't matter, though. If the person were anyone from Justice, they'd recognize me. I'd know the voice. I did not.

This was bad.

But being trapped upside down in a crashed car was likely the worse of the two options the situation presented me with. "I'm...stuck."

"Yes, I'm fully aware of that. We're going to get you out, though."

Cool. Good plan. Get me out. Elijah was out.

Oh hell, Elijah. "Where's my brother?"

The dark chuckle that filtered through the car did not instill confidence.

"He was the easier retrieval."

I had no idea what that meant, but it didn't matter. Someone was outside, someone I didn't know. Someone I couldn't trust but had to because there was no easy way for me to get out of the situation I had found myself in. Whether being in the car or out of it was more dangerous, I had yet to know. I assumed in it.

As the sound of more voices from outside grew, I braced myself for one hell of a headache and opened my eyes. Phone. I needed to find my phone. Even Elijah's would work—I knew his passcode to unlock it. Anything to get in touch with Deacon or Alder or one of the guys in town. Anything at all.

There was nothing on what should have been the roof of the car but blood, a few pieces of paper, and what looked like glass.

Mostly blood.

I had no idea if it was mine or my brother's.

I needed to get to Elijah.

It took four men, a lot of yelling, and some sort of tool that made my head want to explode while it was running for the people outside to access me. I hung in place the entire time, trying so hard not to think about what was to come. Hoping against hope that someone from town would happen to drive by. Would see. Would call for help.

All hopes that didn't come to fruition.

"Here we go, Lainie," the man outside said as he reached in and sort of cradled my shoulders. The fact that he knew my name wasn't lost on me, but I wasn't about to ask him about it because at the same moment, another man grabbed my hips and pushed me against the back of the seat while bringing a knife toward my neck.

I may have whimpered. I may have also allowed a single tear to fall. When the knife sliced through the seat belt and I was caught by all the hands reaching inside, I may have even sighed in relief. It was not a long-lived feeling.

"Keep her steady," someone yelled. Hands all over me, gripping, tugging, flipping me around. Everything spun even when I wasn't in motion, though I was almost always in motion. Eventually, I ended up sitting in the back of a van. What my friends in Denver and I called a murder van—one of those panel vans with no windows. The kind that, if it parked next to your car in a dark parking lot, you would walk back inside and shop some more until it left, instead of having to step beside it.

I was inside of one.

And so was Elijah.

"Eli." I tried to reach for him, but the world spun out of control when I moved and I started to fall. Big, strong hands caught me.

"Easy there, honey."

"I'm not your honey," I spat, the answer automatic. Not that I could do anything about someone using a term of endearment I didn't like. I could barely hold my head up enough to look at the guy.

But when I did, his beard moved with what had to have been a smile, reminding me of Gage. "I was told you Kennards were tough stock. Apparently, that came through for the female as well as the males."

Not Gage but bearded like him. And totally unfamiliar to me. "How do you know who I am?"

He brought what looked like gauze and a cotton ball soaked in some sort of orangey liquid to my forehead, his hands in gloves like a doctor or an EMT. "We've been keeping an eye on you."

My blood went cold, and I hissed as whatever he was rubbing on my head caused a stinging sensation to burn into my flesh. "Why?"

He looked me square in the eye, that grin lifting his beard again. "Gotta know your enemy."

Another man walked up behind him with a phone in his hand. My phone if the edges of the case—gold and glittery, something I'd thought was fun at the time—were any indication.

"Speak."

I stared at him, unable to make sense of the command. He sighed and shoved the phone closer.

"Speak. Now."

Oh. So, like a dog. Got it. "Woof."

His hand made contact with my face in a way that I'd never experienced, and I fell to the side. The world exploded once again, colors and lights and the sound of blood rushing through my ears blocking everything else out. The man with the phone—the one who had hit me—was yelling something into the device. The other—the doctor one—simply stood to the side, leaning his big shoulder against the open van door. Watching the yeller.

Me? I was simply trying to stay conscious. I was also trying my darnedest not to vomit all over myself. Spinning heads did not make for settled stomachs.

A grunt from across the van broke through the noise, though. One from where Elijah lay.

"Eli," I whispered, suddenly refocused and trying to claw my way to him. "Eli, wake up."

"He's hurt pretty bad," the doctor guy said. "I doubt he'll talk back to you."

I looked his way, frowning. "Where'd the other guy go?"

Beardy shrugged. "Off to fight the world, I suppose."

"You're not a fighter?"

"Oh, I am. But I happen to think some fights aren't worth the collateral damage that'll come with them." He gave me a hard look, one with meaning behind it that I couldn't understand. "You Justice folks have been giving us hell for months, and fighting back doesn't seem to be the answer. Others don't want to accept that, though."

I laughed, the effort exhausting and painful. "My brothers won't ever give up protecting their own. It's in their genes."

A cough choked me, forcing its way out of my body in a violent sort of way. The taste of blood filled my mouth as I lay there with pain and colors exploding in my head. Every move, every jerk in response to the action I couldn't stop, was more painful and dizzying than the last. The doc reached in and handed me some tissue to spit into, at least. That was about the best I could hope for. Still, I had to try.

"My head really hurts."

He looked me over, his eyes intense. "You hit your head something fierce during the rollover. My bet is you've got one hell of a concussion, maybe even some other trauma."

Trauma. Yeah, that seemed about right. The accident certainly felt traumatic to me.

"And my brother?"

He flicked a glance over my shoulder, his lips tightening. "He's got it worse."

That statement twisted my gut and brought tears to my eyes. "Please. He needs a hospital—please let us take him to one. Anyone from Justice would do it. We don't have to call one of my other brothers—"

"It's too late." He leaned closer, dropping his voice. "They're already on their way."

"What?" I said, the horror of the situation growing within me.

He shrugged. "The big bosses want the fight with your town over, so it's going to end today one way or another."

"Are we..." I licked my lips, the dizziness not helping the nausea roiling in my stomach. "Are you using us as bait?"

But I knew the answer already. Especially when I heard the sound of trucks rolling up. The roar of engines likely belonging to my brothers, my friends. My Deacon.

The doc must have noticed too. "Looks like the party's about to start."

I had seconds left to try, mere moments to get anything done. "Please. One of them will take Eli to the hospital. Don't just sit here and let him die."

But the doc shook his head, that almost-kind expression gone. He looked at me as if I were something scraped off the side of the road, anger and harshness drawing deep lines on his brow.

He looked at me as if I were nothing.

"He probably wouldn't make it even if we did send him now. Just like our friends and brothers never made it back from Justice." He spat to the side, cracking his neck and looking past me. Over me. Through me. "It's time for a little payback. You'd better start praying for yourself instead of worrying about him."

And with that, he turned and walked away, his steps growing quieter the farther he moved. Leaving us behind in the back of a van to die. I couldn't give up, though. Couldn't stop trying to save Elijah. So, I clawed my way across the floor, every movement making the world spin, every twist another incitement for my traitorous stomach. I made it to Elijah's side without throwing up, but only barely,

"Come on, Eli. You have to stay with me." Sniffling, using every ounce of mental energy I had left, I pushed myself up to sit beside him. The view took a rough, sideways trip then circled around, not helping the sick feelings. But then it righted itself, and I was able to see what was coming through the windshield at the front of the van. The number of bikers pitted against my family. The trucks belonging to Alder and Bishop, Gage and Zane facing off against the bikes and cars. Coming into the fight headfirst and wide open.

I grabbed Elijah's hand and held on, my entire body quaking.

Certain we were all about to die.

Chapter Twenty

DEACON

Y ou've fucked up, son. You fucked up big-time."

The guy on the other end just laughed. "I don't think so, but you hold on to that bravado if it works for you. You did tell us to send you an invitation, remember?"

The night they'd come up on Lainie and me in the truck. They sure had, which meant the man on the other end of the phone was likely the one I'd called mouthpiece. Motherfucker.

"I remember, all right, but I doubt your ass is at Applebee's right now." I signaled to Zane and Camden to stay quiet, switching the audio to speakerphone. "Where's Lainie?"

"She and the one brother are with us."

Camden jumped up, rushing toward the ammunition room down the hall. The backup stash to what was already in the bar.

I had to stand still or I'd throw the damn phone through the wall, which wouldn't help anyone. "I want to talk to her."

"Of course. Hold, please."

While waiting, Camden came out carrying a box. He went back and repeated the action. Emptying the room, it seemed. Stacking options up in the bar area. Prepping us for whatever was coming, which looked to be war. I was going to have to thank him later.

The man on the other end of the phone suddenly spoke again, sounding farther away than before. "Speak."

My stomach dropped, my entire body curling over the device as it lay on the bar. Listening for anything that sounded like my girl.

"Speak. Now."

Still not her. But then.

"Woof."

Relief flooded me, and I nearly smiled. At least until I heard what sounded like a slap over the line and a feminine grunt. My Lainie had just made a sound of pain. The world went red.

"Did you fucking hit her?"

"She was being obstinate."

My eyes met Zane's, his expression a mirror of the absolute rage burning through me at the very thought of someone laying their hands on that woman. My woman. "You're dead."

"Yes, yes. You're a big bad military man and will kill me. I got that. But listen, before we get to your silly pipe dream, I want Alder Kennard. Now. Every minute you delay is another minute I allow your friend and her brother to inch closer to death."

Ice took over the raging heat, freezing me into place. "What do you mean, closer to death?"

"There was an accident, see," he said, sounding almost giddy. "They need medical attention."

"If she dies—"

"I wouldn't worry so much about her. It's the brother who seems to be slipping away with every second. Maybe we shouldn't have hit the car as hard as we did. The flipping was quite fun to watch, though."

I caught Zane's eye at the mention of Elijah, watching as the color drained from his face. As his expression changed from fear to panic to flat-out death lord. Camden looked at me with black eyes, a shark in the water ready to strike. A zombie on the hunt. Zane looked at me with the eyes of a demon, absolutely filled with hellfire and hate. Alive and burning. Camden was going to kill the man who murdered his wife. Zane was going to strike down that entire crew and raze the ground they dared to step onto if Elijah met the same fate.

And I was going to join both of them because the same motherfuckers had dared to put a hand on my girl.

"You've made a huge mistake," I said, still watching Zane. Practically basking in the heat of fury the man was giving off.

"I'm dead. Right. Got it," phone guy said, obviously not aware of exactly what or whom he was up against. "We're close to the halfway point between your bar and town. You can't miss us. See you in five."

With that, he hung up. I stared at the phone, momentarily frozen. So fucking worried about Lainie. I wanted to roll up on them like a SEAL, to go in guns blazing and bombs detonating. I wanted—

"We need a plan," I said, interrupting my own thoughts because I knew they wouldn't get me what I wanted. "Get Alder on the phone."

Camden dropped his phone beside mine. "Already done."

"Deac," Alder said, the fear in his voice obvious even through the device. "Bishop and Gage are two minutes out from me, then we're rolling that way."

Zane piped in from beside me. "My team is on their way. I've got medical support—three of them. They'll be solely focused on getting to Lainie and Elijah." He gave me a strong look, one that imparted confidence. The devil doing what he was good at with his team of demons beside him. "We will take care of the two of them. You're needed in the air."

In the air—as in up and in sniper mode. Likely in the tree line. My brain balked at first, wanting to get to my girl. To protect her. But then the training I'd gone through kicked in, all the years of fighting and planning and working within enemy groups descended. He was right—my place was up high.

"I need an exact location so I can come up through the forest."

Zane nodded, smacking my shoulder in a congratulatory way. "We'll have that in two. Alder, you and your team show up. Negotiate. Whatever it takes. Know that mine will be backing you up, as well as getting Lainie and Elijah out of there."

"Roger that. Going to earpieces, frequency one."

Earpieces—so we could communicate. So we could hear one another and share information. Ours had multiple frequencies so teams could work together but keep some conversations off the main channel. High-tech as fuck and with a long-range for service. That gave me an idea.

"Understood. Be online in three." I tapped to end the call then rushed to the back room, tossing boxes and containers to the floor as I hunted for what I needed. There, in a metal case labeled US ARMY, were the extra earpieces I kept on hand. I slipped one into my ear, bringing the box back to the bar.

"Take one," I said, nodding to Zane and Camden. "Set your frequency to one for Alder." I grabbed another one, slipping it into my other ear. "I'll also be on three."

Zane watched me, his brow pulled tight, obviously confused.

I handed him an extra earpiece set to my frequency. "Get this to her."

Realization slipped over his face, and he nodded. "Elijah?"

I handed him two more, knowing he'd want the same thing. "Put them on four. You'll need to manually switch the main ones to silent so no one else hears you."

He nodded once, pocketing his earpieces on one side of his vest while the others went into his front pants pocket. "Let's load up."

But I couldn't just let him go. I knew exactly what he was feeling, exactly the amount of rage burning him up inside. Exactly the amount of guilt eating at him. I knew, because I felt the same.

"Zane, I know—"

"Load up," he said, ending the conversation. "Elijah and Lainie need medical help, which means I need to meet up with my team before they go in. You need time to circle around and hump through the woods. Camden... What is your plan, Camden?"

The man looked up from where he had been loading ammunition into the tactical belt he'd secured around his waist. Those eyes—so dead and lifeless over the past few days—were darker than usual. His face harder. He'd gone into full predator mode.

"Kill Coyote, slaughter the rest given the chance."

I looked at Zane, neither of us saying anything for a moment. Finally, I shrugged. "Okay...yeah. Sounds good. Let's roll."

* * *

It took all of three minutes to load up and roll out, a length of time that seemed excruciatingly long to me. Still, we needed to take it. Weapons had to be collected and organized for accessibility, safety gear had to be donned. And yet, with every passing second, I could only think of my Lainie...in danger. Alone.

I was going to kill the fucker who hit her. That was a given.

"Ready?" Zane asked as he circled his truck.

I nodded, my sniper gear stowed and ready to go. "You'll text me once your team tells you where they are?"

"Yeah. I expect to know any second now."

"Good. And you've got what you need, Cam?"

The man nodded and gave me a thumbs-up, disappearing into his truck and roaring the engine to life.

"He's a liability," Zane said, watching him roll out of the parking lot.

"Maybe. He's also filled with enough rage to take out the entire club."

"That would draw attention from the law that I might not be able to cover up for you."

I shrugged. "So be it. We don't have time to worry about that right now."

"True." Zane looked at me, his expression growing even more serious. "We'll get them out."

Them meaning Lainie and Elijah. I nodded, knowing we both needed that hope, that certainty. We'd get them out because we cared too much about them not to.

Rescue first, vengeance second. "And then we'll kill all the men who planned this attack."

That dark side of Zane shone through for just a moment, the devil inside showing his face. "I like the way you think, sniper."

Because he thought the same way. Because we both knew lines would likely be crossed today.

Without another word, the two of us separated, both heading to our vehicles. I jumped into the seat and headed out, turning off the main highway onto a back road that circled around and eventually ran parallel to the highway. It didn't follow the entire length of the highway, so I had to hope it would at least get me close enough to hump in quickly. Zane didn't disappoint—I had only just started down the dirt road when he texted me a location. One I knew well enough and could definitely get to quickly.

He then sent me another text.

Med team on the ground. Making contact in three.

"Excellent." I slipped the Lainie earpiece in, counting the seconds in my head.

Ready to talk to my girl before I set the world on fire.

Chapter Twenty-One

LAINIE

There was nothing going on outside of the van. Nothing I could see or hear, at least. Whether my brothers were fighting or negotiating or doing something else I hadn't thought of, I had no idea. But Elijah was breathing, and that was all I cared about in the moment, all I could focus on. Every slight exhale was a gift, every labored inhale a relief. I counted every one, timed them. Kept my body close to his in case he needed to stay warm. It was just Elijah and me in that van. At least until some woman with a halo of hair circling her pretty face appeared at the doors and made me jump in surprise.

Jumping and concussions did not go together.

"Oh." I grabbed my head, the moan I couldn't hold in long and deep. "Damn, that hurts."

"Sorry, didn't mean to surprise you," the woman said, giving me a smile—a true, happy smile. I sort of half rolled, half started to sit up, but she put her hand out. "Two things. One, don't move yet. Two, Deacon sent me."

The relief that washed over me, the pure and utter feeling of safety, was unstoppable. Deacon. My Deacon had sent her. Tears welled in my eyes, and my breath shook as I inhaled.

"Is he here?"

"Somewhere. Zane said he's doing what Deacon does, so I assume that means he's in the air." She glanced behind her before climbing into the van. "Okay, Lainie Kennard—let's do this. I'm Cassia, Zane's field medic, and I need to look you over."

"No. Elijah." I finally pushed myself to a sitting position, fighting against the dizziness that tried to drown me every time I moved. "I've got a concussion for sure, but he's worse. He hasn't woken up since we've been in here."

She looked at me, frowning, obviously concerned. Then she gave me a single nod. "Two seconds with you just to be safe. Look right at me."

I did as I was told, holding still as she shone a small penlight in my eyes. I was quite proud of myself for not jerking away when the light brought with it an ice pick that stabbed my brain.

"Pupils aren't dilated, which is good." She grabbed my wrist, doing that two-finger thing that means they're taking your pulse. "Did the light hurt your head?"

"A little." A lie, and if the look she gave me—upward glance, eyebrows raised, eyes locking on mine as if to say *You sure about that "little"?*—was any indication, she knew it. "Fine. It hurt a lot. Please don't use it again because I'm tired of being stabbed in the brain."

"Yeah, I figured. Deacon sent me with a handgun for you, but—"

"No way. I can barely see straight. I'd be more likely to kill one of my brothers or something."

"Smart decision." Cassia nodded, wrapping a digital watch-looking thing around my wrist. "You must have really knocked yourself in the accident."

"It wasn't an accident."

She went still for a second, continuing to watch the digital screen on my wrist. "Yeah, we know. Habit to call it one." She took the watch thing off and gave me a smile before she grabbed something out of the bag on her hip. "Put this in your ear."

I took the tiny device with a wire dangling from it, more than a little hesitant to put something that looked like a bug in my anything. "What is it?"

"You'll see. Now put it in your ear so I can go check on your brother."

I did as she said, slipping the tiny piece of plastic into my ear as quickly as I could. Elijah needed her attention—the device could have started wiggling and squealing, and I still would have stuck the thing in my ear for him. I assumed the earpiece was a speaker of some sort, but I didn't hear anything at first. I was about to tell her that when she pressed a button clipped to her shirt and began speaking.

"Eagle one secure but without talons. Repeat, without talons based on injuries received. I'm going to need a full team for a medical extraction for eagle two. Male, thirties, nonresponsive. Looks like a massive head trauma." She waited, staring down at her watch as she held Eli's wrist. Taking his pulse that time. "Better call for a bird. He's going to need a Level II trauma center, minimum."

I held my breath, my entire body burning as fear raced through my blood. Eli needed a helicopter to get him out—I'd lived in rural America long enough to know that wasn't a good sign. Helicopters were called when people were dying. Which meant Elijah...

Before I could finish that horrifying thought, I heard something in my ear. A voice through that little earpiece.

"How you doing, beautiful?"

"Deacon," I said, unable not to. Cassia looked up at me and gave me a little smile before returning her attention to Elijah. "Is that really you?"

"It's definitely me. How you holding up?"

I wanted to cry. I wanted to scream about what had happened and sob about how afraid I'd been. I wanted to tell him about every moment I could remember. But the events affecting me weren't important right then. "I'm really worried about Eli. He's not doing well."

"Yeah, I heard Cassia call for an extraction. She'll take good care of you both, and a team is on its way in to get you. We'll get him out."

I nodded as if he could see me, knowing he would live up to that promise. "Where's Alder and the rest?"

"About half a click in front of your van."

It took me a second to translate that, my brain not being too happy about needing to think. "Click is kilometer, right?"

He chuckled. "Yeah. So, they're about 1500 feet in front of you. The bikers are facing off with them—all the bikers that I can see. Seems they pulled you and Elijah from the wreck and assumed you were too beat-up to escape."

I moved in a sort of rolling shuffle to the wall of the van, leaning against it for support. Breathing through the nausea the movement brought on. "They're probably not wrong."

Deacon's voice went harder, more direct. "We're going to get you out, okay? You just have to hang on for me."

"I'm planning on it." I sat in silence, watching Cassia sit with Eli.

She'd slipped some sort of neck brace on him and had him flat on his back. From my vantage, I could see how bad his injuries were. Most of his face was covered in blood, and there was a definite depression on his head. As if...as if he'd been hit by something hard enough to collapse part of his skull.

I was going to be sick.

"Lainie," Deacon said, his voice a little quieter than before. "I'm going to need you to tell Cassia her team is there."

"Cassia," I said, catching her attention. "Your team is here."

She looked out the back of the van and slipped off the edge of the floor. "Thanks."

With that, she rushed off, disappearing behind one of the many cars parked in back of us. Leaving Eli and me alone. I wanted so badly to trust her, to trust that someone was coming for my brother, but I couldn't. My world had flipped completely upside down, and I had no idea how to handle it.

No idea except for one. "Deacon. She left."

"It's okay," he said, that reassuring tone back. His voice a salve over the sting of desertion. "She'll meet her team to discuss options for the safest way to get him out. Just give them a few seconds."

A few seconds was right—Cassia was climbing into the van before Deacon finished speaking, two men right behind her but staying on the ground.

"The second you're clear of the zone of the action, call for a life flight," Cassia said, directing the men. "Tell them he's a Level II trauma patient. He can't go to some country hospital."

The first man nodded, crawling inside the van all the way to Elijah's feet as his partner stood by his head. "Ready in three. One, two..."

And then they were in motion, both men supporting Elijah's

weight as Cassia kept his head steady. Rushing out the back and into the sunlight once more. Disappearing into the parking lot the side of the highway had become.

We were on the side of the highway.

How no one had driven by and seen the chaos was beyond me.

"You okay?" Deacon asked, a quiet sort of comfort in my ear.

"No one's driven past," I said, trying hard not to think about my brother. About the danger my entire family was in at that moment. "I know Justice is small, but there's been no one—"

"They put up a detour closer to town. Alder and Bishop saw it."

"Oh. I guess that makes sense." Though, it didn't. Nothing made sense anymore. Not a damn thing. My head hurt so bad I wanted to vomit, my brothers were standing off against a motorcycle club half a fucking click away, I had no idea where Deacon was except that he could see the van I was in, and Elijah... My god, Elijah. The thought of him, my brother and roommate, my partner in crime in Denver, not making it safely to the hospital he so desperately needed brought out the tears.

Deacon must have heard my breathing change. "Lainie? What's wrong?"

"He looks so bad, Deacon," I whispered, voice gritty and thick. "He got hurt so bad."

"I know, beautiful. They're going to get him help, though. Cassia and her team—they're amazing. I sent them to come get you, which should tell you how much I trust them."

Yeah, it did. He would have come himself instead of sending someone unqualified. I knew that as sure as I knew my name.

I sniffed, wiping my tears and looking out the back of the van at the sunlight-dappled cars and the high grass blowing in the breeze. "Where are you, anyway?"

"Can you step outside? Just past the door."

I crawled my way to the back of the van, the dizziness from moving a little less than before. I wasn't sure if that was a good thing or not, if it was because I was figuring out how to use my body without having my brain revolt against me or getting a little better, but I'd take being able to move without wanting to puke any day. Once I reached the edge, I set my feet down and slid off the bumper. "Okay. I'm no longer in the van."

"Take two steps forward, then turn to your left and look away from the road. I'm about forty yards into the tree line and another thirty in front of the van."

I did as I was told, creeping around the door. Feeling far too vulnerable outside the protection of the vehicle. I looked into the trees in the direction he had told me to. Looked, and saw nothing.

Disappointment hurt way more than I had expected. "I don't see anything—"

A flash. Like a mirror catching sunlight somewhere in the trees. The same sort of flash I'd seen that day in the woods when the man had been spotted on the other side of the ravine. Another flash. Again. Three times. Intentional flashing. I'd never seen anything so beautiful.

This time, the tears falling came from relief. "I see you."

"And I see you, baby. Not long now, okay? Cassia will be back and—" Deacon went silent for a moment before hissing a cuss. "Fuck. Get back inside the van."

I did as I was told, turning and groaning as the world spun again. Moving way too fast but understanding the urgency in his words. From maybe twenty feet away, the doc from earlier—the one from the Soul Suckers—appeared off the back of the van. Rushing my way. Looking positively enraged. I shuffled back, staring.

Knowing he was coming for me. Praying for something to stop him.

Just as I reached the van, as I hopped up to slip inside, a thud sounded through the air. The man jerked and fell, as if the thud had been a punch to the head. He didn't get back up either. For a long moment, all was silent again. Just the breeze and the birds and my own heavy breathing breaking the stillness.

"What just happened?" I asked, not sure if I could believe my own eyes. Waiting for him to pop back up like in some sort of movie.

"You okay?" Deacon asked, sounding a bit more stressed than usual.

"I have a concussion and moving makes me hurt, but I don't think my head is fucked up enough to imagine what I just saw. Was that you?"

"Yeah. One down."

One down—as in dead. As in shot by Deacon. I felt nothing but an odd sort of pride in him for that. "How many more to go?"

"Counting twelve but could be more. I'm just waiting on the signal to start taking them out."

"Who's sending the signal?"

"Alder."

My brother. Which meant more of my family was there, a thousand feet plus in front of the van I was basically hiding inside of.

"Who else is there?" I asked, needing to know.

"Bishop, Gage, Camden, Zane and his team. Our buddy Chase, Hunter from the mill, and a few others from town are on their way to offer backup from the fringes and do any evacs we need. We sent Finn to corral all the women and keep them safe out at Bishop's house. We've got a solid team on our side."

Which was fine, but I was more worried about the ones in

immediate danger. "Alder and those guys—they're just up front? With the bad guys?"

"No. Some are—"

Something sharp and loud sounded through the air, breaking the relative silence of the day outside the van. I was about to ask what that was when Deacon cursed again.

"Fuck. Stay down, Lainie."

More sharp noises—gunshots, I had to imagine. I had no idea what to do, no clue what was happening or if I should be helping somehow. The next time I heard Deacon, it was obvious from the start that he wasn't talking to me.

"Four down, two at your three. Taking shots now." A pause, and the sound of men yelling came from outside the van. "I've lost one. Repeat. I do not have eyes on one."

I couldn't hear a response—whatever channel or item Deacon was using obviously didn't come through my earpiece. But I could hear the panic in his voice, the worry. This was bad.

"What can I do?" I whispered, not wanting to interrupt him but wanting to help. He didn't answer me. Unable to sit still, I crawled to the back of the van and slipped over the edge. Bracing myself for the spinning I knew would happen. Hanging on to the door to keep myself upright as I got to my feet once more.

"One in retreat mode. Fucker slipped behind a car. I have no eyes on him. Repeat. I have no eyes on him."

I peeked around the door of the van, moving away from where I knew Deacon was. If someone was hiding behind cars, they had to be on that side, right? My brain felt fuzzy, but that made sense—keep the cars between you and the big gun in the woods. Yeah, if I were trying to hide, that would make total sense.

I kept my back to the van and inched forward. Keeping an eye out. Moving slowly and deliberately. I was at the front bumper when the idea of being like Deacon—of getting up in the air—occurred to me.

"This is going to hurt," I whispered to myself, almost in preparation for what I knew I needed to do. Clenching my jaw and fighting back nausea, I climbed onto the hood of the van. I kept my eyes on the metal and glass, kept my head slightly down as I continued up. As I tried not to notice the way everything spun around me. I simply kept putting one hand in front of the other, one foot bearing my weight before I dared to move the other. I inched my way up, only stopping once I was kneeling on the roof. I made the mistake of looking over the grassy field around me, the movement battling hard with my head injury. Nausea finally won that battle, and I threw up over the side of the van, the pressure making the pain even worse. Unable to hold it in any longer. But I was determined not to fail. Deacon needed help, which meant my brothers were in danger. I had to do something.

"Lainie, what the fuck—"

"I'm helping," I said, wiping my mouth on the back of my hand before surveying the area around me. "You said one, and you said hiding behind cars. I'm going to be an extra set of eyes."

"Get back in the van, Elaine."

Oh. I really did like it when he used my full name, but not like that. "Call me Elaine when we're not alone and naked again, and you'll be sorry."

"Lainie," he said, sounding really stern and angry. "You need to get—"

"Blue truck," I said, spotting something moving up ahead. "Man behind the blue truck about fifty yards in front of me."

"I swear to god, woman. If you don't get back inside that van—"

"Blue truck!"

The man had stood up and started running my way. He didn't make it far. Without much sound at all, without a single sort of warning other than a repeat of that funky thudding sound, he jerked to the side. Blood spread down his face as his eyes met mine, a look of surprise I could see from where I sat. And then he fell.

"Two down," I said, letting my head drop and my shoulders sag.

"Can you please get back inside the van now?"

"Yeah. I think I can." I was about to slide off the roof of the van when all hell broke loose again. Suddenly, there were gunshots coming from what sounded like everywhere. Men began to run, some stopping behind the vehicles parked on the side of the road. Some using the cars for cover to hide, while others used them as cover to shoot. Which meant they were shooting at my brothers. I had never wished to be holding a gun more in my life.

"Deacon."

"Working on it." His voice shifted, the words no longer meant for me. "Looks like five on the run, possibly six. Alder, you've got company behind the silver coupe on your three. Anyone got a better shot?" A pause. Silence on my end. "Shifting positions. Give me two minutes, and I'll see if I can take him."

I looked toward where I knew Deacon to be, hoping to see a flash of something. A little sign that he was okay. I had no idea what was going on ahead of me except it sounded dangerous.

And I was sitting on top of a van. Out in the open.

"You're an idiot, Lainie."

"You're the furthest thing from an idiot, beautiful," Deacon said, his voice a little more strained than usual.

"Ha-ha." I slid down the windshield of the van then across the hood. The ground seemed suddenly so far away, and I knew any sort of landing was going to be brutal on my head. "This is going to hurt."

Maybe I should have been more descriptive about what *this* I meant. Maybe I should have said something like sliding off or hopping down. I didn't. I said something was going to hurt, and that apparently caught Deacon's attention.

"Lainie, what are you—" There was a grunt and then a sound that made no sense in my mind. An almost pained sort of groan. I froze, turning slowly in the direction I knew him to be. Waiting for something—anything—to make those sounds make sense.

I received nothing.

"Deacon?" I finally said, almost whispering. Too afraid to raise my voice. "Baby?"

A hiss and then he was talking again, though not to me. "Shot. I've...been shot. You have no cover."

I was off the van without thinking about the need to move, stumbling hard when I hit the grass and again losing what little was in my stomach. Didn't matter. I finished throwing up, wiped my mouth with the back of my hand, and started moving. One foot in front of the other, just like crawling up the van to the roof but horizontal. Everything continued to spin and swirl, my entire world becoming a scene in some movie about being really drunk or high. I was neither—my brain was hurt and telling me to hold still, but I couldn't listen to that traitorous bitch.

"I'm coming, Deacon."

He didn't answer me, which only fueled the desperate need to get to him. I fell twice, puked a few more times, and dry heaved more times than I could count, but I kept moving. Deacon needed me. No concussion was going to stop me from getting to him.

Pity to the person who tried to get in my way.

Chapter Twenty-Two

DEACON

"Two down," Lainie said, her beautiful voice so tired in my ear. I didn't have the heart to tell her I was at eight—she didn't need to know how much death I'd caused.

"Can you please get inside the van now?"

My girl didn't argue. For once. "Yeah. I think I can."

Thank the heavens. I took a look over what had become a battlefield, watching for any sort of skirmish or firefight to start again. Alder was in full negotiation mode with the leader of the group, his deep voice demanding the crew leave Justice and never come back or he'd keep taking them out. Bishop and Gage were playing hide-and-seek with a couple of bikers on the far side of the field. I had no shot, but I kept watching.

Apparently it was Camden I should have been paying attention to.

"Fuck." I aimed toward the man Camden had flushed out of a

hiding spot, but the angle was all wrong. Gunshots sounded across the field again, and my focus split between all my guys. I would take anyone out—if a Soul Sucker got into my sights, they were going down. Zane's group was backing us up like the fucking professionals they were, but these bikers were still trouble and they'd really set up a labyrinth of a battlefield. Between all the parked cars, the tall grass, and the trees themselves, they had far too many places to hide from us. But a good battlefield setup wasn't enough to stop me. I'd find those fuckers and take them down one by one. I wasn't losing a friend today.

Lainie came through my earpiece, whispering my name at the same moment Zane popped up in my other one.

"Got three on the east side behind the silver coupe, one with a long-range rifle. Gonna need you to take him out."

"Working on it." I twisted as much as I could considering I was lying lengthwise along a fucking tree branch. "Looks like five on the run, possibly six." I'd thought there were twelve total, but these bikers just kept popping up like roaches. Multiplying practically before my eyes. "Alder, you've got company behind the silver coupe on your three. Anyone got a better shot?" Four voices sounded almost at once, not a single one giving me an affirmative. Which meant I was the only one who had a chance at taking out the threat. "Shifting positions. Give me two minutes, and I'll see if I can take him."

I shimmied across the branch to the trunk of the tree, tugging my Kevlar vest back into place once my feet were on the ground and shouldering my rifle. I needed to move about fifteen yards south and then get back in the air. I didn't usually like to change positions once I'd set myself up—too easy to become a target—but this was a necessity. Alder needed me, and I really needed these bastards to die so I could get Lainie the hell off the battlefield.

Speaking of my girl, her voice—a little distracted-sounding—came through the earpiece on my left. "You're an idiot, Lainie."

I chuffed a laugh and grinned, looking toward the van. Moving quickly through the tree line as I tried to stay behind cover. "You're the furthest thing from an idiot, beautiful."

"Ha-ha." She paused, giving me the chance to run between trees. I made it to the one I wanted and began to climb, more vulnerable than usual because of my movements. Once I got on the branch, I'd be good. Harder to find. Right now...

"This is going to hurt."

I froze almost flat on my stomach, whipping my head in the direction of the van. "Lainie, what are you—"

Suddenly, I was in motion, falling both down and back as if I'd been pushed. My brain couldn't keep up with what was happening, not quite understanding what stopped my momentum so fast and why my neck and chest had started to burn. Nothing made sense. At least not until I raised my left hand and saw all the blood.

Running on pure instinct, I pressed the button on my wrist—the one controlling my right earpiece. The one that opened the channel between me and my team. Praying everyone got the message in time.

"Shot. I've...been shot. Fucker must have gotten me in the neck." I coughed, the words hard to get out. My throat filling up with something that sent a shot of fear up my spine. I wouldn't abandon my team, though. "You have no cover."

And then I fell back, staring upward. Doing my best to keep my breathing steady even though it hurt like a son of a bitch to do so. The canopy above me danced in the breeze, dark green and peaceful. Sounds quieted, and the light from the sun grew dimmer. Darker. The world began to disappear as my body moved into a state of shock. I knew the signs, knew the damage that could be done if I didn't stay awake and keep myself grounded outside of the pain. I couldn't move, couldn't breathe without feeling like my chest was on fire. Things were bad. Dire, even.

But the only sounds in my earpiece were of the men on my team. If I was going to die, if this was the end, that wasn't what I wanted to be hearing. Shaking, fighting against my body's revolt at the motion, I reached up and tugged my right earpiece out. I needed to focus.

"Lainie," I said, licking my lips. Hearing the drag in my voice. The gurgle in my chest. Fuck, this was bad. Whoever had taken that shot at me had aimed well because my vest would have protected me if I'd been standing. Too bad I'd been lying down on that branch. Too bad that shooter had been good enough to pop me right in the space where my shoulder met my neck. Bad area to be shot for sure, which meant I was running out of time. "Beautiful, my lungs hurt, and I'm pretty sure I'm going to pass out soon."

Nothing. No answer. No response. It was like I was talking into a void.

And if I was, I was laying it all out.

"You'd better be safe, beautiful. Don't...make me come back from the dead—" deeper breath and a little cough that made me moan as pain exploded over me "—fuck...come back to haunt some asshole who should have known not to put his hands on you." I took a deep breath, growling through the pain of it and curling slightly onto my side. "Dammit, breathing shouldn't be this hard."

"Deacon." My girl sounded panicked and tired, but I was so damned happy to hear her. "Hang on. I'm coming."

I huffed a laugh, coughing at the end, the metallic taste of blood coating my tongue. "Not much to hang on to at this point, beautiful. Even breathing's getting a little tricky."

"Don't you give up, you jackass."

"Never." But I closed my eyes, trying hard to put as much of my strength into my voice so she could hear me. Truly *hear* me. "I love you, Elaine Kennard. Whether I call you Lainie or Elaine or beautiful, it doesn't matter. I love all of you. If we get out of this alive"—*which felt like a true* if *in that moment*—"I'm taking you to that beach. We're going to get married with our feet in the sand and the waves in the background. You hear me?"

But I had a feeling I was the one who couldn't hear her. There was a roar in my ears, the sound of my own blood pumping causing me so much pain. I just needed to close my eyes for a few. Just needed to rest for a minute so I could regain my strength.

Just needed to get one more thing off my chest before I accepted the darkness clawing at my periphery.

"I love you, beautiful. You're everything to me."

And then the world went dark.

Chapter Twenty-Three

LAINIE

You're everything to me.

That was the last thing I heard from Deacon. He'd said he loved me, that he wanted to marry me, and that I was his everything. Then he'd gone silent.

"Fuck you, Deacon," I whispered as I finally hit the tree line. Needing to hang on to the trunk of one to stay upright. "You don't get to say all that mushy stuff then die on me."

"Lainie." Camden came rushing toward me through the trees with Zane right on his heels. "Where's Deacon?"

I pointed, still not super stable. "Over there somewhere."

"On it." And then he was gone, leaving me alone with Zane. A man I'd barely spoken to. The man who had been dating my brother, apparently.

"He's bad," I whispered. Not sure how open he was about his personal life. "Elijah. He's so bad."

Zane grabbed my arm, directing me to a tree stump and trying to get me to sit down. I pushed him off and kept walking. Stumbling, really, but moving forward.

"Gotta get to Deacon."

Zane followed me, quiet. Silent, actually. The only way I knew he was even there was because he would occasionally grab my elbow and help steady me on my trek. Otherwise, he didn't say a word. Until he did.

"Cassia said you refused to be evaced."

It took me about three seconds too long to put his words together. Evaced...evacuated...taken to the hospital.

"Elijah needed it more."

Another period of silence, more helping me traverse the woods. Another surprising moment when he actually spoke again.

"Thank you." Soft. Barely more than a whisper. So much emotion behind those two words, though.

I glanced his way, squinting because the sunlight was behind him and it stabbed me in the brain to look that way. "He's my brother. As are you now, it seems."

He smiled and huffed in an almost embarrassed sort of way, nodding toward the forest. "I can see Camden kneeling. We're almost there."

"Deacon," I said, the sound almost an instinct. Moving faster to meet up with Camden, whom even I could see through the shadows. "He needs me."

"Yeah, he does. And the whole crew now knows it."

I paused for just a second, my gut sinking. "Sorry?"

"He had both channels open there at the end. No more hiding for the two of you."

I gave that a solid thought as we came upon a scene out of my nightmares. Camden knelt over Deacon's body, my love's shirt torn open and his skin covered in blood. His lips were the wrong color—too pale, almost blue—and his skin was as pasty as I'd ever seen. But he was breathing. Barely.

Jesus, we had been so stupid. "Hiding the fact that I love that man is the least of my worries right now."

"We're going to need to get him out of here!" Camden yelled.

"That's going to be a problem."

I turned at the unknown voice, coming face-to-face with six men. They wore black from head to toe, had a symbol on their vests that looked a lot like the Soul Suckers patches under curved banners with words on them, and had guns pointed at us. Big guns. I may have been gun-knowledgeable, but I wasn't a gun expert. What they carried looked like military rifles. Ones that fired hundreds of shots per minute. We were in trouble.

Zane grabbed my arm and tugged me behind him. "You don't want—"

He didn't get to finish his statement. Camden stood, his hands covered in blood, and pulled a gun from his hip holster. He was still rising when he fired, still focused on one guy—one particular guy—as he moved into firing position. His shot landed clean—straight to the forehead. The man never had a chance.

His friends did, though.

Three of the four pointed their guns at the boy I'd grown up with and fired. I'd been right—those guns fired a ton of bullets in a very short period of time. Camden jerked back and forth, gun dropping from his hand, arms flailing. And then he fell beside Deacon. Silent. Still.

Too still.

"Cam," I said, moving toward him out of habit. But Zane had an arm around me and was practically carrying me in a different direction. He shoved me behind a tree and pressed something on his wrist.

"Cease fire!" someone yelled—presumably one of the bikers—and the world went quiet again. Or mostly quiet.

"Two men down," Zane whisper-yelled while holding a button clipped to his shirt. "Cam fired into a crowd. We are under siege. I repeat, we are under siege."

But we weren't. Not really. The guns had gone quiet, the men no longer firing at us. The woods sat silent for a long moment, the tension thick but fading.

"We're not going to kill you!" the unknown voice from the other group yelled. "Not unless you're an idiot like that one and shoot at us. Come back from behind there. I need to have a conversation with you."

"You stay here," Zane whispered, looking at me with a firm, don't-ask-questions expression. "I mean it."

I nodded, leaning against the tree and knowing I was flat-out lying to the man. Accepting that I was about to do something that could likely put me in danger, not that I'd ever gotten out of it. Still, I could have used a little family support because my brain would not allow me to follow Zane's direction.

As soon as Zane moved, so did I. While he edged around the tree and forward, closer to where the other men stood—guns now pointing at the ground—I headed to where Deacon and Cam were. They needed someone to take care of them. I was about to become that someone.

"Tank, how is he?" the man asked, his eyes on Zane and his gun hanging at his side. One of his men—presumably Tank—attended to the guy Camden had shot. He didn't look happy when he sat back on his knees.

"Coyote's dead."

Coyote. As in the man who had killed Leah. No wonder Cam had started shooting so suddenly.

I hurried to where Camden lay in the grass, grabbing his hand and feeling for a pulse. Feeling nothing. Moving my fingers along his wrist and trying to remember how Cassia had held hers over mine. A quick glance at Deacon told me he was breathing, so I had a few minutes to focus on Cam. He seemed the most damaged at that moment.

"One of yours killed one of ours," the leader of the Soul Suckers group said. "That leaves us uneven."

But those men didn't matter. I had two on the ground, and they needed me to care about them in that moment. They needed me to make sure they were alive and breathing—

Breaths. I had to check for breaths.

I leaned down to listen with my ear against Cam's lips. Praying for something. Desperate for the sound or the feeling of air against my skin. Of anything.

The universe gave me nothing.

The tears came of their own volition, making my eyes burn as they began to fall. Making my own breaths come in choppier and less even. My friend was dead. Laid out on the forest floor in a pool of his own blood. He'd fulfilled his mission at the end—killing the man who'd murdered his wife.

Something Zane obviously knew and understood.

"He killed Coyote as payback. That man helped murder his wife." Zane didn't sound scared in the least. He had an earpiece where my brothers were likely talking to him, so I took his confidence as knowledge of the firepower coming. Or he was a really good liar. Either way, it didn't matter. I kept my head bowed over Camden, kept letting the tears fall unbidden.

"You did it," I whispered, knowing that moment must have given him so much peace. Finally. "You killed Coyote. Leah's death is avenged."

Because that's what he'd done. He'd given up his life to close that chapter of his story. To seek retribution for what they'd done to his wife. He'd paid the ultimate price for vengeance, and I couldn't say it had been the wrong decision for him.

"Seems you people in Justice like killing my men."

My men. As if we hadn't lost as well. I turned, lifting my head. Taking a better look at those outfits and patches. Was this some sort of national president? Was this a big leader of the Soul Suckers and not just a random club president? The Medusa with all his individual clubs as the snakes?

If so, he needed a good beheading.

"We don't enjoy it," Alder said, appearing almost out of nowhere. He wore camo nearly head to toe and had a look about him that I'd never seen before. A rough one, solid and sure and downright mean. The man before me was someone I didn't know and who actually scared me. This wasn't my brother—this was the soldier who'd spent years defending our nation, and he was there defending me because he'd heard Elijah and I were in trouble. He'd come running in full gear and armed to save us.

Talk about a gut-check moment.

"You must be Alder," Medusa—because that was how I was going to see him from now on—said. "I've heard a lot about you."

Alder crept forward, Bishop appearing behind him. The three

men—Zane and my two brothers—suddenly making a triangle shape.

"I don't know shit about you except that you're on Justice land and have just killed a Justice son. Feel like explaining what the fuck you're doing here?"

Deacon coughed. He *coughed*. A sound that stole every bit of my attention. Still tearing up, my heart breaking that I had to let go of Camden's hand, I crawled closer to Deacon. His eyes fluttered but didn't open, and his hand was moving in a way that seemed like he was trying to grab something. Like he was reaching. I put mine in his.

"Shh. It's okay. We're going to get you out of here," I whispered, trying hard not to garner attention. Failing miserably, it seemed.

"You have a man down and a woman who obviously needs medical care." The man flicked a glance my way, one quickly blocked as Bishop took a step to stand more fully between us. That didn't stop the man from talking, though. "You're still outnumbered, too. We can help you."

Alder didn't even appear to flinch. "We have a man down because of you, and that woman needs medical care because of your sidekick. You can find his body on the road, by the way. No one puts their hands on a woman in my town and gets away with it. Especially not *my* sister."

A little sexist, maybe. A little overbearing, probably. But I was damned happy to hear him say the words anyway. As strong as I was and as independent as I knew I could be, having someone who would always defend you in the worst of situations was a gift. One from a brother I had been neglecting.

"Oh," Alder said, sounding really happy with himself all of a sudden. "And we're not outnumbered."

The snap of a stick breaking caught my attention, and I looked up to see Gage leaning against a tree just past me. Two other guys—I had to assume from Zane's group since I didn't recognize them—flanked him. We were at six big, armed men to their five. Refusing to be left out, I reached down and grabbed the handgun Deacon had strapped to his hip. Then I sat, one hand holding Deacon's and the other holding the gun, facing the enemy.

Deacon and Zane had once commented on the fact that they thought I had the Kennard big dick energy. In that moment, I would have agreed with them. And I was full-on swinging it around.

Medusa noticed. "You don't want to do that."

Alder practically leaped forward, gun raised and pointed right at Medusa's face. Blocking the man from seeing me at all. The tension in that little patch of trees flew up right along with his arm.

"You don't talk to her. You don't look at her. She's not involved in this."

"Word on the street is there *is* a woman involved in this, though. One who it seemed started the entire war we're now engaged in. One who betrayed her Soul Sucker family." He paused, the silence lingering. The tension rising. Until finally... "Tell me, Alder Kennard —how's your wife doing?"

Oh hell.

That was the end. I knew it, the other guys knew it, even Medusa knew it. The expression on his face shifted subtly as he attempted to stare down my brother. He went from cocky and arrogant to surprised to downright scared in a matter of seconds. All the while, Alder stood stock-still, not moving. Not firing his gun. Not even saying a word.

At least, not until Medusa tried to backpedal. "I understand you may—"

"You understand jack shit," Alder said, his voice low and deep. A tone I'd never once heard come from him. "This is how this little moment of yours is going to play out. You're going to pack up this ragtag team of thugs and drive them the fuck out of my town. Hell, you're going to drive them out of my county and state. You're going to keep driving until you get back to where you came from. Then you're going to forget we ever existed. No Soul Sucker comes within a hundred miles of Justice, or they die. Period." He moved forward, not slowing when the men behind Medusa raised their guns. "And if you ever even think about my wife again, if you whisper her name in the silence of a sanctuary, I'll take you out like Camden just took out Coyote. Don't think for a second that I won't die for my woman."

I was watching Medusa's face for a reaction, which was how I missed Deacon waking up. One second, the man was flat on his back, barely breathing, with my hand in his. The next, he was sitting up and had an arm around me. Leaning on me for support.

"Hush," he said, his voice super weak. "It's just me."

"I thought you were dying."

"I think I am, but I owe your brother something."

He grabbed my hand—the one with the gun—and raised it. The weakness I felt in his grip, the way he was using my body to support his, worried me, but he never faltered. He brought our joined arms up, ducked his head so he had it fully resting on my shoulder, and he moved our linked hands until he had the gun pointed right where he wanted it.

Which was not anywhere near the men facing off with my brother.

"Shoot," Deacon said, sounding more tired than I would have thought.

"What?" I asked, the word not making sense.

"Now. Shoot. Pull the fucking trigger."

Closing my eyes, too afraid of the outcome to look, I did as I was told. I pulled the trigger and fired the gun. Deacon fell back to the ground, taking me with him. Gun still in our hands and his breaths coming in pants. I opened my eyes to see a man on the ground a good ten feet behind Medusa and his crew. One I hadn't even noticed. One I doubted any of us had noticed except for Deacon.

"Where did he—"

But I didn't have time to ask the question I needed to because we went from nothing to battle in a beat. Medusa's men dropped and ran and began to fire. Alder dove behind a tree, rolling into a position where he could lie on the ground and fire. I clung to Deacon, covering my head and waiting out the noise. Hoping and praying our men made it out alive.

That we all survived this day, unlike Camden.

Eventually, the forest was silent once more.

"You two okay?" Alder asked. I opened my eyes and looked down the length of Deacon's body, nodding slowly. Alder glanced over my head. "Everyone all right back there?"

"We're good," Bishop said. "What the fuck was that? Why'd Deacon shoot?"

"I have a good feeling that I know." Alder rose to his feet, creeping closer to where Medusa lay. In fact, all the Soul Suckers were flat on their backs. He kicked Medusa's arm. "You're not dead. Don't play possum on me."

Medusa rolled slightly, giving me access to his expression. He certainly seemed injured. "You killed my team."

"Damn straight, I did. Good call having a sniper in the trees. It's something I would have done—that's a smart move."

Medusa choked on a laugh, blood running down his chin. "Now

what? You're just going to kill me and assume the Soul Suckers won't come looking for us?"

"Nah, son. I'm going to take you to a hospital to get you looked at, and then I'm going to give you a choice."

"What kind of choice?"

"Well, you see, that man over there—" he pointed at Zane "—he's the county undersheriff. And you just enacted a plot to kidnap two locals, killed another one, and shot a beloved business owner. Maybe you're not afraid of jail time, but I bet you're not fond of it."

"So, what's the choice?"

"We take you for medical care, you get the fuck out. Period. Forever. Like I said before—a Soul Sucker comes within one hundred miles of Justice, we kill them. I'm going to alter that, though, since you were trying to kill me while we were in a good faith negotiation. Any club comes within a hundred miles, we kill them."

"I can't control other clubs."

"You sent the Black Angels here, so that's not quite true. You put the word out, and I bet people will listen. And I'm going to up the ante for you too. Any biker comes within a hundred miles of Justice, not only do they die, you do too. Because we see one more motorcycle in this part of the country, and we're going on the offensive. We'll take y'all out—families, too. So, make your choice, son. You got thirty seconds."

"Fuck you." Medusa coughed, a spray of blood exploding from his mouth.

"You might want to try a different answer," Alder said, placing his booted foot on Medusa's throat. Leaning his weight forward and looking way too casual for what he was doing. "Let me put a little pressure on that wound for you. I don't think coughing up blood is a good sign."

The man on the ground grabbed my brother's ankle, his legs moving as if to kick but not with enough force. Finally, Alder eased off.

"Well?" Alder said, practically growling the word. "Got another answer for me?

"Fine," Medusa spat, groaning as he rolled slightly onto his side. "I'll put an order out. No one will come near Justice."

"Good man." Alder stood, looking as if he were about to leave the man behind, but turning back at the last moment. "Oh, and don't even think about trying to breach this verbal contract. I don't care how many years from now, if I see a motorcycle on my highway, I'm coming for you. As you can see—" he waved an arm around the field where six dead Soul Suckers lay "—we don't miss."

Medusa nodded, coughing up more blood. "Fine. I agree."

"Good." Alder looked to Zane. "Call for a couple choppers. We've got four needing life flights."

"No," Zane said, already on his phone and tapping the screen. "Three."

"Why only three?" Bishop asked.

"The prez over there, Lainie, and Deacon." With that, he turned away, talking fast into his device. Moving away from the upcoming fallout that was going to be bad. So very bad.

It was Gage who asked the question I knew would be coming. The one I was the only person who could answer in that moment. "What about Cam?"

I shook my head, still holding Deacon's hand. Fighting back new tears. "Camden's dead."

Every head turned my way, all the people fighting on the side of Justice looking absolutely devastated.

"No!" Bishop yelled, rushing over to Camden's body. Pushing Zane out of the way as he ran. "Fuck, no. We didn't lose him, too."

But we had, and the rest of the team already knew it.

Bishop's shoulders dropped when he pushed his fingers against Camden's throat, obviously not feeling a pulse in his veins. A cry of anger left his mouth, and he shuddered in what could only be described as a physical representation of grief. Gage knelt beside him, arm around my brother. Both men breaking under the weight of the loss.

So much loss.

Alder slipped in beside me, sliding his big arm around my shoulders. "You okay, sis?"

I nodded, unable to find words. My brother wrapped me up in a hug, though. He supported me in that moment of weakness, giving me what I needed. No bullshit, no demanding, no manipulation. Just one sibling holding up another.

The weight of knowing how many of Alder's hugs I'd missed out on over the years slammed into me, exacerbating my grief. Falling right into place as my adrenaline crashed. I began to cry.

It was Deacon's voice that soothed me, though. "Don't cry, beautiful."

I jerked from Alder's arms, bending over my love. Feeling my heart jump when he smiled up at me. It looked painful—that smile —but I'd take it all day.

"How are you doing?"

Deacon coughed, a little blood showing up at the corner of his mouth. "I was shot in the neck, and I'm pretty sure my lung is collapsed. I'd really like some morphine and a good, long stay in a hospital right about now."

I ran my hand over his forehead. "Zane's calling for choppers. We'll get you help."

"Seven minutes out," Zane said, still kneeling over Camden's body. "And I've got my team coming to deal with cleanup. They'll take Camden to wherever he needs to go."

"Molnar's." The word came from all of us at once—Alder, Bishop, Deacon, Gage, and me. There wasn't anyone else we trusted to care for our dead but the old, family-run funeral home in Rock Falls. It was where we'd waked our parents, where we'd cried together before their burials. Camden would have wanted his service there... and then he would have wanted to be buried with his love.

Zane didn't seem surprised by our selection. "Okay, then. To Molnar's he will go. Six minutes out."

I gripped Deacon's hand that much tighter, counting down the seconds in my head. Praying for his health and safety. The wait for the helicopters seemed brutally long, but eventually, the thump-thump-thump of their approach broke the relative silence of the woods. Gage and Bishop rushed out to guide them to our spot. Meanwhile, Alder sat beside Deacon with me. Silent.

Until he wasn't.

"You took a bullet protecting me."

Deacon opened his eyes and looked at my brother, his face completely serious. "I did."

Alder tapped a spot on his ribs with two fingers. "I took one for you, and you took one for me. We're even now."

I had no idea what they were talking about. I never knew Alder had been shot. But apparently my love did.

Deacon coughed and raised his arm, the two men grabbing hands in some sort of physical contract. "Good. Now you can start paying for your bourbon."

Alder chuckled just as two medics came rushing through the trees toward us. He whistled loud and pointed to Deacon. Then he glanced at me.

"You okay being second?"

I nodded, already used to feeling nauseated from the motion. "Of course. Deacon's more important."

Deacon grabbed my hand, his eyes glazing over slightly as the medics moved into position and started checking him for vitals.

I was in the way. "I have to move," I said, bringing his hand to my mouth to kiss the back of it. "You're going for that hospital stay now, and I'll be right behind you."

"Your head..." He closed his eyes as the medics moved him, shifting a board underneath him. Preparing to carry him out.

"The only thing wrong with my head is you won't leave it."

"Good." He turned my way as the medics lifted him, giving me a weak smile. "As soon as I'm up and moving again, we're heading to a beach and getting married."

And then he passed out.

Chapter Twenty-Four

DEACON

Time had a tendency to stand still in hospitals. Blinks of consciousness pressed against my memories, small moments of light and dark, of noise and silence. I came to, understanding where I was and remembering why I was there, at least. How long I'd been out was another issue entirely. Whether I was out of it for two days or two weeks, I had no idea. All I did know was the pain was pretty intense when it finally pulled me from sleep.

"Motherfucker," I said, hissing and rolling slightly to the side. Trying to move away from what hurt. It didn't help.

"That's going to make it worse," Alder said. I popped open my eyes, more than a little surprised to hear him. Shocked to actually see him.

"What are you doing here?"

My best friend and the man who may now want to kill me

because of my relationship with his sister walked around the bed, finding and pressing a button on a cord.

"I'm making sure they treat you like the fucking hero you are." He put the button thing in my hand. "That's for your morphine drip. It's not unlimited, but it'll give you a little hit if you're in pain and the timing is right."

He walked back around the foot of the bed. I got a real good look at the man as he did. A real good one.

"You look like shit. What the fuck crawled on your face and died?"

Alder chuckled all low and deep. "Pretty sure I've heard that one before."

Yeah, he had. And not all that long ago. Though the day we had first met up with a biker to figure out what to do about the Soul Suckers, the day we'd brought Parris—now Chase—into the Justice family. The day we'd truly kicked off this war we'd been waging against the motorcycle club seemed so many lifetimes ago.

Or maybe just lives.

"All the arrangements made for Cam?"

Alder sighed, his face falling a bit. Looking even more tired and raggedy than I'd ever seen him.

"Camden. And Elijah."

I swear, my heart stopped. Just for a second, just enough to make a machine sound some sort of high-pitched alarm. It stopped, and then it started again at a rate that likely wasn't good for me. I didn't want to believe it, didn't want to accept what I'd just been told, but looking at Alder cemented his words as truth. Eyes red, cheeks flushing, he was in torment. A man fighting hard not to break down in front of others.

"Alder. Brother..."

Alder's head fell forward and his shoulders sagged. There were no words to share, no way to take the pain away. I'd lost a good friend, a man I respected and truly enjoyed spending time with. Alder had lost a brother. There was no comparison. Yet if my grief—that crushing, burning sensation that tore through my chest and turned my gut molten—was even half of his, I'd be surprised. Alder had to be carrying one hell of a heavy load in that moment.

And there was nothing I could say to ease that burden.

"I'm so sorry, man. What can I do? What do you need?"

Alder shook his head, surreptitiously wiping his face with his hand before taking a deep breath. "We're taking care of everything. Camden had a will, or at least a final letter he kept on him. He wanted to be cremated and buried with Leah. Zane pulled some strings for us because exhuming a body is apparently a big fucking deal. We did everything quick—got him cremated, had a tiny ceremony at the graveyard, and put him with Leah. It's where he always should have been anyway."

Awful. Everything about that situation was awful from the start. Camden and Leah hadn't deserved the ending they'd received. They were both good people, happy people. A couple that truly loved each other.

"And Elijah?"

Alder sighed again, staring out the window across the room. "We buried him next to my parents. I've never seen Lainie cry so hard."

Lainie. My beautiful princess, alone during such a trying time. Well, not alone. She had her brothers. But still—I hadn't been able to be there with her, something I already knew I'd regret for the rest of my life. That sort of guilt wasn't something you just walked away from.

Which brought my mind around to another subject.

"How's Finn holding up?"

"He's struggling hard, but Lainie, Shye, and Jinx are holding him together. Those are some strong-ass women." He shook his head and sighed, taking a seat beside my bed. "You have any idea how long you've been in here?"

I had to really think about it. Had to count the number of times I could remember waking up. They didn't make any sense, though. "Not a clue."

"Three weeks. You've been unconscious or near enough not to make a lick of sense for over two weeks. And during that time, you died three times." He shot me a look, steeling me in place with angry blue eyes. "The only reason there aren't fifteen doctors and nurses in here right now is that you woke up for a short bit last night. Do you remember that?"

"No." And I didn't. Not at all. I also didn't remember dying.

"Good. It's been a shit few weeks."

I sighed, my eyes already heavy. I wasn't ready to go back to sleep yet, though. "I missed Thanksgiving."

He chuckled under his breath. "We all did. There wasn't much celebrating going on—Lainie ended up bringing all the food here to feed the nurses. Pretty sure you got extra sponge baths after that one."

I almost laughed, but the pain it caused cut me off short. "Not sure I like the idea of being naked and unconscious around a bunch of people."

"Don't worry about that—Lainie was here every day, making sure you got the care you deserved." He sighed and leaned forward, staring at the floor as he brought his hands together. "You and my baby sister, huh?"

Fuck me. I was not in the shape for this conversation. But

apparently, there was no avoiding it. There was also no sidestepping the facts. "I love her, man."

His jaw clenched and released, clenched and released. "She told me I'm an overbearing prick."

"You can be."

"I don't want to lose anyone else. Not my sister, not my best friend. None of you get to fucking walk away from me."

"I didn't plan on going anywhere."

"Except an island, so you can marry my sister."

"We'd come back eventually."

"And if she wanted you to move to Denver with her?"

I gave that statement the consideration it deserved, knowing that was actually going to have to be brought up with Lainie at some point. "I'll make her come visit. A lot."

"She might fight you on that."

"I don't want to lose another brother either, Alder," I said, holding his eyes and making my meaning known. Making sure I reinforced our connection and friendship. "We'll figure it out—I'll work with her."

"Well, you might not have to work too hard."

"Why's that?"

"She's moving home. Said she wants her family around her. And with Elijah gone..."

She'd be alone in Denver. Oh, my poor, beautiful princess. "I missed a lot."

"You did, lazy fucker. Just had to lie here sleeping while we dealt with the fallout from the fight."

"Anything I need to—"

"No. Not a damn thing. I've got it covered." He shook his head, looking out the window. "You almost died out there. I'll deal with making sure that warlord motherfucker stays gone."

"Is that who he was?"

"Yeah. National Warlord."

"Like Cartel."

"Who's Cartel?"

"Someone Chase and I had to deal with."

"You never mentioned that to me."

"Only way to keep a secret is to keep your mouth shut."

Alder nodded, letting his head drop again. "I know Zane and Elijah were a couple. And I know you knew."

Oh. "That wasn't my news to tell."

"Never assumed it was. I'm just glad he found a little joy before..." He looked out the window, breathing harder. Obviously needing a moment to collect himself. "Zane isn't handling it well. The man looks like a nuclear bomb ready to drop."

That actually wasn't surprising in the least. "And he has nowhere to take out that rage."

"Yeah. I don't think he's going to stick around much longer. He's got that wild look in his eye, you know? Like Camden had before he took off."

The look of a man burning alive from the inside. I remembered the look well.

Alder sighed again, looking my way. Really staring hard at me. "I don't think there's anything we—"

A nurse chose that moment to come in, smiling at me. "Mr. Manns, the doctor is going to want to talk to you soon." She glanced at Alder, the smile falling. "You've got three minutes."

Alder nodded, locking eyes on hers and not backing down. Waiting for her to leave before he stopped glaring in her direction.

"What was that about?"

He shrugged. "They don't like me telling them what to do."

"You told them what to do?"

"I told them they had to save your scrawny ass every time that fucking monitor went flatline. There may have been yelling. I almost got kicked out one night for cussing." He sat deeper in his seat, crossing one ankle over the other knee. "I already lost one brother—I wasn't losing another one."

I held out my fist to him, taking his bump when he offered it. Knowing that was the highest praise I'd ever get.

And needing to redirect the conversation. "How is Lainie?"

Alder sighed again. "Man, it's been rough. She didn't just have a concussion—she has a traumatic brain injury. The doctors—and there've been a fuckton of them—aren't sure what long-term effects it will have on her."

"What do you mean?"

"I know she wants to tell you, but you need to be prepared." He sat back, shaking his head. "Like, if she walked in here right now, she'd seem totally normal. But there are moments when her eyes unfocus or she loses track of a conversation. She gets headaches a lot. Doc says it's all part of the healing but that her brain may not be able to handle certain things anymore. She might forget how to do basic skills."

That sounded awful and so very scary. I was going to cuss out my own body for leaving me unconscious when she needed me so badly once I was able to stand up and look myself in the mirror. "What kinds of basic skills?"

"Nothing super drastic. More like...little things. Weird things. Doc said he's got one patient who is totally fine except she can't tell time on a clock face anymore."

My response was immediate. "I'll buy her all digital clocks, then."

He looked my way, a small, sad smile gracing his lips. "You would, wouldn't you?"

"Of course."

He bumped my fist again. "Cool. Because she's outside, waiting to talk to you."

I turned, my eyes going immediately to where the nurse had appeared. Alder stood and walked across the room, disappearing down the small hallway that led to the door. When he came back, he had Lainie by his side. My God...

"You are so fucking beautiful."

She laughed and rushed over, grabbing my hand immediately. "It's good to see you awake finally."

I reached up to run my hand over her forehead, pushing her hair back. "How's the brain?"

"Broken, but so far not in too much of a jagged way. How's the lung?"

"Fuck if I know, but it doesn't hurt to breathe." Of course, at that point, nothing really hurt. In fact, my head was starting to spin a little. Morphine was hitting me.

And apparently, Lainie recognized that. "He's getting sleepy."

I nodded, suddenly so fucking tired. I wanted to stay awake, to sit with her. To hear all about what had happened once we'd left the forest. Wanted it so bad.

"He needs his rest," Alder said, and I wrenched my eyes open and shook my head. Clinging to Lainie's hand so she wouldn't disappear again.

"Nah. I'm fine."

"You just fell asleep there, son. I think it's time for us to go so you can rest again."

I didn't let go of Lainie. "Please don't."

"I'll stay with him for a bit," she said, her voice soft and exactly what I needed to soothe the ache inside me. "Just until the doctors are done with him."

I shook myself awake, needing to stay conscious for a few minutes more. Knowing that there was so much more I needed to say and do. To atone for. "Yo, Alder."

"Yeah, man?"

I gripped Lainie's hand tighter. "I love your sister. I love her so much, and I'm going to marry her the second she lets me."

Alder glanced at Lainie, smiling. "Yeah, I know. We all do."

Lainie laughed and leaned over my bed, whispering, "Your frequency on the earpieces changed when you fell. The whole team heard that final speech."

Oh. Ohhhhh. That made everything almost seem better. "Well, good—then they all know you're mine."

"Yeah," she said, running her hand over my hair and gifting me the most amazing, beautiful smile in the world. "They all do."

I was fully okay with that.

Alder crept up beside me just as a doctor walked in, leaning down to say goodbye. Or so I thought. I was just tired enough not to brace myself for his movement, not to be prepared when he grabbed my arm and tugged me a little closer to him. When he started talking in a cold, deathly still voice that meant business.

"I heard your proclamation of love and it was the sort of thing I'd say to my Shye, so I'm not going to be angry that you were with my little sister behind my back. We'll ignore that fact because she's an adult who can make her own damn decisions and she chose to chase your ass." He moved a little closer, his voice dropping. "But if you ever even think of hurting her, I'll make sure there's no medical team around to hump your ass out of the woods. Best friend or not—that's my *sister*. Do you understand me?"

There was only one answer for that statement, one way to get across exactly how much I understood his intentions.

"Hooah."

Lainie looked a little confused as Alder rose to his full height, but he ignored her expression. As would I. Some things were meant to stay between men. Or at least, not to be brought up around little sisters who found their overprotective older brothers unbearable. Let them fight over something else.

Before he left, Alder gave my shoulder a squeeze and addressed the doctors. "He's awake and pretty well lucid. He was in some serious pain when he first woke up but used his morphine button. I'll leave you to it, but my sister..."

Lainie shook her head. "I'm staying."

Alder shrugged. "She's staying. She's got a wedding to plan with this lug."

I gripped Lainie's hand tighter as Alder disappeared down the hallway. Leaving me alone with doctors and nurses...and the love of my life.

"Pick a beach, beautiful," I said, the words sounding muffled and thick even to my own ears. Sleep creeping up on me quick. "Just pick a beach."

Epilogue

LAINIE

I was made to sit on a beach, drink a pineapple daiquiri, and bask in the sunshine. There was no doubt in my mind. The sound of the waves in the background, the smell of the ocean air drifting by, and the feel of the sun warming my skin? Made for it.

"I'm going to run in to make an old-fashioned—want another drink?" Deacon asked, rising from the chaise lounge next to mine and stretching that glorious body of his. I looked him over as I had a tendency to do, relishing every muscle and dip, every inch I'd been blessed to explore. The tanned skin he'd been showing off on the daily with me. His scars were healing, and he only expressed the pain from his being shot when he was moving in certain ways or exerting himself too much. Whether we had a lot of sex with me on top was from his injury or simply because he liked watching me ride him, I would never know. I didn't care either.

I bit my bottom lip as I watched him, waiting for him to bless me with that smile. The one that was solely mine, the one that said he knew where my mind had gone and was thinking the same thing. The one that made his green eyes burn like fire.

I giggled when I finally got it. "No thanks, baby. I think I've had enough."

He rolled his eyes and headed for the house, whistling along the way. I lay back and let myself revel in the warmth and the overwhelming feeling of happiness that I'd been living with since I'd gotten Deacon out of the hospital. I wasn't saying life had suddenly become all rainbows and unicorn kisses, but it was pretty damn close. I'd finished my degree, moved home, and started working on repairing the fractured relationship between my two older brothers and myself. Finn and I had always been solid, but I made sure to really put energy into my relationship with his girlfriend, Jinx. I had tea with Anabeth and coffee with Shye, too. Losing Elijah—

I laid my hand over my chest, even thinking his name still so very difficult and painful.

Losing Elijah had taught me really quick that I didn't have a day to spare when it came to loving my family and friends. The burial of Camden had been heartbreaking but almost...comforting. He'd finally escaped the pain he'd been living in and had made his way back to his Leah. There was a peace in that to temper the loss.

Burying Elijah had not brought any sort of peace. There had only been loss and anger that he'd been taken from us so soon. That we'd lost him so suddenly and in such a violent manner. I'd cried for four days straight after his funeral. My brothers had all come to sit with me, to mourn with me. To grieve together as a family. We were still grieving all these months later, but life had begun to move on in fits and starts.

I'd come home, storing all of Elijah's stuff in Alder's barn for safekeeping. Elijah had left me his house, and the sale of it had given me a nice little nest egg to live on while I figured out what I was going to do as a career in such a small town. Alder and Shye had surprised us all with an announcement that she was pregnant—hence why she'd seemed so tired and almost sick the week of Thanksgiving. Anabeth grew practically every day, her belly getting bigger each time I saw her. Bishop was the happiest I'd ever seen him, and he spoiled that woman as much as he could. They were a joy to be around. Finn and Jinx had run off and gotten married without telling anyone, which really hadn't been a surprise. Those two were free spirits and bound to set their own rules. The Kennard clan was building a new generation, something to be joyous about. But everything we did was tinged with the sadness of Eli's passing.

Even my own happiness.

Finn wasn't the only one who'd said I do recently.

My new husband returned, drink in hand. Sunglasses covering his eyes. Not that I couldn't tell he was looking right at me, that I couldn't feel his hungry gaze. I smiled up at him, still surprised that he was mine. That we'd rushed so much to tie ourselves to each other. That we were both still healing in a lot of ways but had chosen to heal together as a unit. He was a gift I hadn't been expecting, and I would never forget the peace and love I'd felt on the day we'd made it official.

"How you feeling, beautiful?"

That was a question I got on the regular. It wasn't meant to be rhetorical or a greeting of some sort—it was Deacon checking in on me and my damaged brain. His *How you feeling?* meant *Does your head hurt?* because headaches were something I suffered from. It meant *Is your vision wobbly?* as mine sometimes got. Meant *Does anything in your body feel tingly or disconnected?* a sign we had learned meant I needed to rest. Deacon's simple question was never simple, but there were plenty of times when I was able to give him a simple answer.

"I'm feeling good. I'd be feeling better if you were closer, though."

My Deacon never left me wanting for a single thing—not a drink, not a blanket, not a hug or a kiss.

The man dropped down, settling his knee between my legs and bringing his body to rest on mine. Covering me and giving me what I wanted in spades. I wrapped my arms around him, absorbing his warmth as I smiled up at him. Running one hand over the scars from where the bullet had entered his body and where the doctors had been forced to go in and retrieve it. He ran a finger over the scar on my forehead, the one that would likely never go away and I had no real way of hiding. The one that I'd gotten when something—we never would know what—had crashed into my skull during the car accident. We were a mess, my new husband and I. A mess positively made for each other.

"How'd I get so lucky?" Deacon whispered before pressing a soft kiss to my collarbone and snuggling in, lying right on top of me. Cuddling me. This had been something I'd only just learned about the man—his need for affection. He was very tactile—always grabbing for me, tugging me close, holding on to me. I loved it, even in the middle of the night when he woke me up to roll me partially underneath him. There was a sweetness to the act, a protectiveness I couldn't deny enjoying. It was why his no-furniture cabin worked so well for us—we'd fall into the pillows and stay there, constantly grounded in touch with the other. Legs and arms intertwined at all times.

We didn't live there, though. Deacon had moved me in to his

other house, the one in town. The one with real furniture. But we spent a lot of time at the cabin, just us and the pillows.

Comfy but wanting more than just a snuggle, I lifted my leg and wrapped it around his hips, tugging him closer.

"Whatcha doing, baby?" he asked even as he rocked his hips into mine.

There was no use playing coy with him. "Seducing you. Is it working?"

"Doesn't it always?"

He rolled us a little, moving so we were in that perfect sort of position with him on top of me. My legs spread around his hips. The bikini I wore offered almost no coverage, but that didn't matter. Neither did the fact that Deacon tugged the strings of my top until they gave, pulling the slips of fabric from my body and tossing it across the patio.

We were alone.

And about to be naked.

"Deacon," I said, groaning the second syllable as he rocked his hips into mine. Teasing me. He laved at my breast, tugging the nipple between his teeth and flicking his tongue against the tip. Driving me crazy. Making me writhe beneath him.

"Let's head inside so I can fuck you again," he said, mumbling into my neck before he bit down. I loved when he did that, so I groaned and arched into him. Digging my fingernails into his shoulders. But heading inside wasn't a necessity. We were in a bungalow on a private beach at a resort I couldn't have pronounced if I'd tried. I'd told Deacon I wanted him all to myself for our honeymoon week, and he'd come through. We had a butler who brought us food and whatever else we needed and a lovely older woman who cleaned for us some mornings. Other than that, no one bothered us. They couldn't even gain entry to the beach or the little pool off the patio only we had access to. The place was blissful, as was making love to my new husband under the afternoon sun.

"Let's flip over so you're on the bottom and I can ride you right here in the sun."

Deacon chuckled and grabbed me, doing as I'd asked. Flipping us both over until I was sitting astride him. He grabbed both my thighs and pulled them farther apart, letting go of one so he could slip a hand into my bikini bottoms. Keeping his other on my thigh so he could hold me in place. Teasing me even more.

"I think you're secretly a little bit of an exhibitionist," he said, glancing over my shoulder. "Anyone could pass by on a boat out there."

I shrugged, rocking my hips in time with his motions. Reaching down to untie the strings of my bikini bottoms so he could have full access to me. "They won't see anything even if they did. Besides, I don't get off on them seeing anything. I just like the look of your skin in the sun."

And I did. The man tanned like a champion. He also knew that I liked the sound of the waves in the background. The noises in the room—any inside space, really—had a tendency to make me uncomfortable. My doctors were working with me on it, trying to figure out what exactly caused the sensations and anxiety so we could find a way around it, but the process had been slow and disheartening. It wasn't easy to hear that all the things you felt were wrong in your head may never right themselves, that the tiny skills you no longer had may never come back. From my inability to focus my eyes on anything close up to my reduced attention span, the balance issues that sometimes appeared out of nowhere to the way the sound of electricity in the walls made my skin crawl. All small yet terrifying changes I needed to adjust to.

Deacon understood all that and stood by my side through every appointment and occupational therapy session. He worked with me to improve what we could, soothed me when I lost my temper at myself, and was unfailingly patient with me. He never made me feel as if something I couldn't figure out how to do was a problem. He simply accepted my new limitations and worked with me to minimize their negative effects on me. He was a good man.

One I'd married on a hillside with my brother and his best friend presiding over the ceremony.

"Beautiful," he said, grabbing my attention once more with a pat to my thigh. Looking up at me with that patient smile.

I shrugged, grinning. Knowing he had been patiently waiting to reclaim my attention if he was at the point of giving me a love tap. "Sorry. I got distracted."

"If my finger is on your clit and you're distracted, I'm doing something wrong." He gave said clit a rougher nudge, making me jump and moan. Making me grab his chest and refocus on all the delicious ways he had to tease my body. "What were you thinking about, Mrs. Manns?"

"You. Us." I leaned over, placing a kiss on his lips. Rocking my hips against where he was already so hard for me. "How wonderful you are. And how amazing our wedding was."

He chuckled, kissing me back. Both of us laughing over the wedding that almost hadn't happened. Alder may have accepted the fact that his best friend had fallen in love with his little sister, but that didn't mean he'd made it easy on us. Even after he'd agreed to become ordained solely so he *could* marry us.

But that was a story for another time because my man had my

hips in his hands and was rolling his body into mine. Teasing me. Making me wet and ready and so damn impatient for him. Finally, I pushed away from him and lifted up onto my knees, tugging his board shorts down to his thighs. Not even stripping him before wrapping my hand around his length and holding him against me. We didn't need to wait. I simply settled on top of him and let him slide inside. Using my own weight to guide the depth.

Deacon groaned and gripped my hips harder, moving me in a way that must have made him feel good. Rocking and lifting me while still keeping one thumb attached to my clit.

"Love you, beautiful," he said as I dropped my feet to the ground and really started riding him. And he did. I knew it, my family knew it, the whole damn world may have known it. Deacon made sure to both tell and show me how he felt about me, and he had no qualms about public displays of affection. Our wedding may have been quick, but it had been right.

He was my husband, my sweet soldier, and the only man I would ever love.

He'd almost died for me.

And there was no way I would ever stop trying to repay him for that.

Kristin Harte started off as a chemistry major in college but somehow ended up writing romances featuring ex-military heroes and the women who knock them to their knees...literally and figuratively. She likes drinking in the shade, snuggling under a warm blanket on a cold evening, and researching how to blow things up. Her children know nothing of what she writes, and her husband just hopes he's not at their Chicago-ish home the day the government shows up to confront Kristin about her Google search history.

When not writing good men doing bad things, Kristin can be found writing paranormal romance as Ellis Leigh, co-writing naughty novellas as London Hale, or taking her signature style into the mystery realm as Mille Thorne.

www.kristinharte.com
Kristin@KristinHarte.com

www.ingramcontent.com/pod-product-compliance
Lightning Source LLC
Chambersburg PA
CBHW030144200726
48285CB00006BA/2002